FROM DEATH ON THE STYX

The attendant, a portly frog-daughter of Heqet named Carla, tells them to report to dock two to board the *Danse Macabre*.

There is some confusion as Frankie attempts to ask what exactly is the *Danse Macabre* and why aren't they reporting to dock one for the *Stygian Jewel*.

The attendant croaks something about pennies and then calls for the next in line.

"It's your lucky day, Eloise," Frankie says. "We've been upgraded."

"I'm still dead. How is that lucky?" Eloise replies.

ALSO BY J. LYNN CARR

VALKARIA MYSTERIES

Wish You Were Here

The Little Cabin

WILD ROOTS COLLECTION

A Werewolf in Mims

Griffinwood Close

For all of the wayward souls.

"No one can hurry me down to Hades before my time,
but if a man's hour is come, be he brave or be he coward,
there is no escape for him when he has once been born."

- The Illiad

LIFE
SOULS TOWN
DEPARTURE
LOUNGE
DEATH

PROLOGUE

Cotton Candy

Frankie Hart will die when she turns eighteen. The deadline looms over her, the days fading fast like water slipping through outstretched fingers. Her parents feel it too.

Despite their acceptance of (and, indeed, enthusiasm for) the inevitable event, they award her an immense amount of autonomy in compensation for the otherwise abundance of life she would be afforded if only she hadn't been born a Hart witch. What does it matter if her stockings are torn, or she misses curfew by an hour if she will only experience eighteen years of life? Who cares if she has ice cream for breakfast, or she spends all of her allowance at the arcade when she has only roughly six thousand five hundred seventy four days to do so?

She has thus far spent her twelve years of life partaking in a certain extent of indulgence that most of her peers, particularly her friend, Beau Astor, look at with unbridled jealousy.

Beau, of course, doesn't know the reason her parents are so ready to forgive her indiscretions, regardless of their size and consequence. He envies her easy smile, her dirty fingernails, and her non-existent curfew.

One would think that Beau could be just as free, just as easy-going, if only for the fact that life feels so immensely big at that age, so full of promise and exhilaration.

There are few concerns to burden his slim shoulders, his heart full with the sheer magic of simply being alive. He is at the start of his journey, and the end is so far in the future, it fails to be an inevitability. He *should* feel as equally unmoored as Frankie. Death is a myth. An ancient language he will never learn. It isn't *real*—much like the social ladder his father likes to tell him about.

But that ladder, as well as his eventual demise, and along with things like time and taxes, are entirely adult fabrications.

Beau's father seems unaware of this truth that Beau sees so clearly. Indeed, Mr. Astor insists on the ladder's existence almost daily and most certainly weekly.

And while Beau finds it easy enough to fake indifference, the words still manage to find their way into his thoughts, his father's voice echoing in his head when he least expects it or, quite frankly, wants it. They rest on those slim shoulders of his, almost like physical things—an ugly, itchy sweater he'd rather not wear. So, Beau is far from untroubled, despite his age of almost thirteen and three-quarters years old. He is not as prone to laughter as Frankie and much more likely to give into fits of sullenness that he feels are entirely justified in the face of Frankie's freedom and his own lack of such.

However, this doesn't impede their friendship. In actuality, there are times when it even seems to help it grow, moments when Frankie's smile can wipe the frown off Beau's face, or when Beau's seriousness helps Frankie concentrate long enough to advance to the next level on that one particular arcade game, the one she's been playing for a week straight, every day after school.

On the first day of the Little Spark Summer Fair, Beau's father prattles on about something or other (the words "responsibility" and "one of these days" are in attendance), while Beau stares at the tall man who he will one day, probably, resemble. For now, however, Beau gets his looks from his mother. He is tall for his age and slim with a well-cut jaw and a long nose. His curly hair is light brown but has already begun to turn darker, toward the mahogany-black that adorns his father's head. When his father finishes his lecture, Beau says, "Yes, sir. I understand, sir."

His father nods and disappears into his study, the door of which is more familiar to Beau than his father's visage. Beau is late to meet Frankie at the boardwalk, but he takes his time making his way out of the house and to the garage, ensuring his helmet is strapped on tight before mounting his bike.

But the Summer Fair calls to him, and he pedals fast, sending a silent wish to the wind for assistance. His legs are jelly when he arrives at the Little Spark Boardwalk. He locks his bike up to the metal palm tree that marks the entrance and pockets the key in the neon bag slung around his hips.

The air smells of fried batter, ocean, and coconut-scented sunscreen. The brined wind coats his face even before he walks up the steps to the main thoroughfare. The fair is bustling with people, but

Beau slips between the crowds easily, invisible by virtue of his age.

He spots Frankie waiting by the arcade, her glasses reflecting the blue sky briefly before she turns toward him, as if she can sense his gaze. She's always doing things like that, giving him little looks and tiny, knowing smiles as if she can see the future, as if she knows what he's about to say or even what he's thinking.

He hopes she can't actually hear what he's thinking. He would be mortified if she knew how often he thought about her.

Her mouth spreads into a smile, her lips tinged blue from the candy she has stuffed into her cheek, and she throws her arms around his neck, hugging him tightly. Her voice is muffled by the candy, but he understands her fine as they begin to strategically plan out their route through the fair.

He forgets his father's lecture entirely. He forgets himself. He forgets the fair, to be honest. Years later, he will only be able to recall Frankie.

Her laugh. Her shoulder as she bumps him after he makes a particularly good joke. Her sharp elbow jutting into his side when he begins to look sullen. Her lips, still blue—only from cotton candy now—pressing against his own when he offers her the goldfish he wins.

Soon, the talk from his father will come back to him. The words will remind him not to do foolish things with foolish girls. The words will draw lines around his days, shaping what has hitherto been blissfully amorphous.

He will find himself under increasing scrutiny from his family, his teachers, his girlfriend, and his football coach. Expectations will be placed on him time and time again, that ugly sweater becoming his daily uniform.

Beau will wear these well. He will walk, straight-backed through life, navigating the maze of expectations with ease until his death, whenever that may be. But for now, he is unaware of what's to come. He is giddy with life. With Frankie. With the

Summer Fair, and the boardwalk, and the ocean beyond. He blushes and licks his lips, tasting her sugar-spun kiss, knowing, despite his age, that he would rather die than live without Frankie Hart.

CHAPTER 1

ROOM 349

Beau looks pale, Frankie thinks, but of course, the journey into Death hits everyone differently. He sits in a creaky metal chair, head between his knees, and groans.

Frankie hands him a lozenge. "It'll help with the nausea." She pops one into her own mouth, and the ginger-sharpness seeps into her tongue as she looks around.

The office is much like any other office, an oblong space with shabby utilitarian furniture and permanently stale coffee in the breakroom. An inescapable cloud of something that feels faintly like despair clings to the carpet and wallpaper and to the underside of their chairs.

There are desks and partitions spaced at seemingly random intervals, but, upon closer inspection, Frankie realizes the arrangement of workspaces is not random. Rather, it is designed to accommodate a diverse workforce, like employees with spiked tails hunched over typewriters, assistants with wings softly humming in the background, and fish-tailed clerks with water tanks installed underneath their desks.

A large snake sits in the corner of the cubicle to their left, hissing into the phone. With a grunt, the snake hangs up the phone and turns to his desk mate. "The ghouls who work in Administration have no idea what they're doing. Can you believe..."

A cloven-footed man with pointed ears walks past them with a companion, a black cat walking on two legs.

The man gives his companion an impish smile and says, "So I said, 'Look, I know you're dead, but sometimes you have to live a little, you know?'"

His companion purrs, twisting his cavalry mustache with a long, finely sharpened nail. He begins to respond, but Frankie misses the retort as they walk on, out of earshot. She turns to watch them leave the office, the glass-paneled door swinging shut behind them. The name of the office is painted onto the pebbled glass, and although she is reading it from the inside, she rearranges the letters in her head.

Room 349

Passport Services

Frankie turns back to Beau and sighs. His head is still between his knees, and he lets out a tiny groan.

She drums her fingers absentmindedly against her knee and reflects on how they got here. Beau's hands may be white-knuckled against his knees at the moment, but they were shaking when he approached her at Harley's Cafe. He slid into the chair opposite hers with no invitation (typical Astor behavior, she thought at the time) and asked for her help.

An unlit cigarette wobbled between his fingers while he attempted to explain the series of events that led him there, to her, in a noisy cafe on a Saturday night, despite the fact that their friendship ended years ago, and, especially, despite the fact that he hasn't said more than two polite words to her in almost as long.

Beau's story was jumbled, and his voice was hard to hear over the jazz band playing in the corner. She had to lean across the table to hear him, which only increased her annoyance at being interrupted by him in the first place. The crucial element of Beau's story, however, was that his girlfriend, Penelope Church, was now, sadly, no longer amongst the living.

As the daughter of witches, Frankie Hart was born with mischief—ancient magic passed down by generations past that allows her to bend the rules of Life and Death. It's no coincidence that Beau Astor approached with this issue: he knew she was magic when he approached her as she sat hunched over a tattered leather-bound book, sipping her tea and twirling a strand of her hair in thought.

Indeed, he has had enough run-ins with her over the years to know about her abilities. She likes to think that she always gives as much as she gets, and she is exceedingly pleased to think that Beau might be a little bit afraid of her.

Because, of course, she is *the* Frankie Hart—who cursed him in the ninth grade after he said something discouraging about her nose.

The Frankie Hart—who once whispered something under her breath after he tripped her in the lunchroom causing his lungs to feel like they would burst from lack of oxygen.

The Frankie Hart—who blinked and gave him oozing, painful boils on his face for two days after he said her glasses made her look like a frog.

Yes, *that* Frankie Hart.

And while that underlying fear and uncertainty

is still there (so rife, she can almost smell it), the fact remains that there are bigger, more important matters to see to: his girlfriend is dead, after all, and he's fairly certain it was his fault.

He had no qualms with signing her standard contract, complete with a confidentiality clause that, if broken, would render the deliverable (i.e. Penelope) back to the state it was in at the time the agreement was signed (i.e. dead).

And, really, where would he be then?

Where he is right now, Frankie supposes.

As they sit in the dimly lit space that smells of disinfectant and stale food, the coldness of Death seeps into her bones slowly and consistently, like a clock counting down the time they can spend here before becoming permanent residents.

Tick, tock.

The minutes slide by, and she begins to regret her decision to help Beau Astor. They have been warily circling each other for years, the children of neighboring families that have never quite gotten along, with few exceptions. They are the same age, go to the same school, have sat in the same classrooms, and have taken the same exams. His persistently thoughtless comments about her appearance, her lineage, and even her abilities as a student have had plenty of time to undercut her pride and leave her perpetually bruised (emotionally speaking).

Of course, they were friends once. But high school changed more than just her height, which is why now, at seventeen and three-quarters years of age, she is not particularly fond of him.

Plus, he won't stop nervously jiggling his leg.

She reminds herself that Beau Astor is the heir to a family fortune so large that she can't even really fathom it. She's looking forward to having an Astor in her debt. Really, waiting in this room is a small price to pay in the grand scheme of things.

She repeats this to herself three times, hoping to believe it.

When the lozenge dissolves, Beau sits up. His

cheeks look pinker, and his eyes look brighter, livelier. He is still jiggling his leg, though, and Frankie places a hand on his knee, feeling the warmth of his skin through the fabric of his pants.

"Would you stop that?" she says, her tongue moving around the lozenge.

"Sorry." His fingers clench against his knees to hold them still. But the jiggling starts up again in a few seconds.

She grits her teeth. "Feeling better?" Her sarcasm is lost on him.

He smiles appreciatively. "Yeah, that was a great spell."

She sighs. "It was just ginger."

"Oh."

"Not everything is magic...." Crossing her arms over her chest, she pulls her bulky coat around herself. She may have been foolish enough to help Beau enter Death, but at least she was not foolish enough to enter without the proper attire.

She casts a sidelong glance at Beau, whose leg

is still jiggling. The coat he wears once belonged to her grandfather, a decommissioned military uniform with an embroidered patch on the left lapel that says "Hart." There were other jackets she could have given to him, but to be perfectly honest, she was hoping the raggedly cut mass of patched fabric would make him look...small, dimmed, bowed under the weight of death. At the very least, she was hoping the olive green, so faded it might as well be brown, would somehow draw out the paleness of his complexion or highlight the gauntness of his face, and not just because she is predisposed to think unkindly about him.

While Death is not without color, there is a coordinated drabness to it all—a muted quality as if someone has simply lowered the saturation and dimmed the brightness. The coat is just as drab as Death and, theoretically, should counteract the inherent color of life that Beau, being alive, still possesses. It's important to note that there is no particular amount of danger to be derived from being alive in Death, as long as the trip is kept brief. She has been told, by those with more expertise, that Death isn't quite so monochrome from the view of its permanent residents, but even so, her attempt at lowering the vibrancy of life that both she and Beau give off has more to do with trying to assimilate into their surroundings. It's just not nice to remind the more permanent residents of what they've lost.

And anyway, the coats have an added benefit. It's terribly cold in Death—the deceptive kind of cold that silently eases its way into your body until you forget what warmth is. But, of course, Beau sits in this office as if he were made of sunshine, the frayed edges of the jacket framing his broad shoulders quite nicely, the spent green bringing out the olive undertone in his skin. He looks vibrant, like he is sitting on a beach in southern Italy instead of this dingy, cold office in Death.

Frankie reaches over and pulls on the shoulder of the coat. "Don't sit so straight," she whispers.

Beau hunches his shoulders forward. "Better?"

No, she thinks. "Perfect," she says.

"So where are we again?"

This is the third time he's asked this question, and she's running out of ways to phrase the explanation. "We're in Death. Sort of."

"And Death is a real place?"

She shrugs. "Mostly."

"So, we're in Death, and we need to find Penelope to bring her back."

"Yep."

"But we got stuck at the border." A pause. "Because your passport is expired?"

She grits her teeth. "Yep," she admits.

After all, she must be honest with herself. She knew her passport would be expiring soon but kept putting off the renewal. The deadline snuck up on her, as deadlines so often do.

"Why do you have a passport for Death?"

Finally, a different question, she thinks, relief flooding through her chest. Maybe this won't be so bad after all.

"I'm a Reaper-in-Training," she says lightly. "I only have one month left for my certification."

"So that's why we're here, in this office? To get your passport renewed?"

"Indeed."

"And after that, we can find Penelope and get out of here?"

The tension gathers again, like electricity amassing before a storm. Technically speaking, there is no way to undo death. Once a soul loses their body, they are faced with a handful of decisions, but becoming alive again is not one of them. There is, however, a loophole that only a select few know about.

Luckily, Frankie is one of the few, being a Reaper-in-Training, and the plan had been quite simple: open the doorway beside Penelope's body, step through, grab her, and pull her back so that her soul could be rejoined with her body. Of course, this plan assumed several things, in particular that Penelope was still standing next to her body, having just died a few moments ago, that her body was habitable, and that Frankie could make the trip with such expediency that it wouldn't register on any official records.

And yet...

Beau had not been entirely accurate in stating that Penelope died in, "I don't know. Like two minutes ago." It had been at least thirty minutes, which is plenty of time for a body to not only become uninhabitable, but for a recently-deceased soul to begin their journey into Death.

To make matters worse, Frankie had quite forgotten that her passport had expired last week. The quick trip was logged and an official summons arrived promptly. The carrier-bat flapped in her face until she took the envelope, which, when opened, transported them here, to Passport Services.

"When do you think Crawfield will show up?" Beau points to the nameplate on the desk in front of them. The desk is exceptionally tidy and would look unused if it weren't for a small typewriter, two stacks of papers, and a coffee mug filled with an assortment of pens. The coffee mug says, "Death's Best Passport Acceptance Agent 1992."

"Soon, I hope," mutters Frankie, looking around the room again. She spots a clock, a faceless white circle hanging on the wall.

Completely useless.

During one of her first sojourns into Death, Frankie asked her instructor why all of the clocks here are faceless and yet still seem to work, a faint ticking sound coming from the depths of the contraption. The instructor, a balding centaur named Darren, shrugged and said, "One of Death's great mysteries. The clocks were installed centuries ago and they can't be removed or changed. Now, for Charon's sake, can we please get back to the syllabus?"

Darren had not liked being interrupted.

"*Brimstone and boils,*" she curses under her breath, wishing she had remembered to wear her watch this morning. The waiting is making her impatient. Beau's leg is still jiggling, and she is seconds away from firmly grasping his knee to again disrupt his movements, when Crawfield arrives, sitting down in his creaky swivel chair with a huff. His attire is far less tidy than his desk, his hair sticking up at odd angles around two tiny horns protruding from either side of his forehead. His disheveled appearance is punctuated by a tiny whirlwind of energy swirling about him, playfully lifting up his tie.

"Sorry," says Crawfield, the sound muffled by his tie. He smooths the offending strip of silk down and holds it to his chest. "The whirlwinds will stop soon. A side-effect of traveling by portal. The vortex was packed this morning. And it's not even rush hour!"

The wind begins to settle as he picks up the top piece of paper on the stack on his desk. "What do we have here?" he mumbles to himself. "Ah, I see." He looks up. "Just here for a standard Passport

Renewal, yes? Are you aware that you might be able to accomplish this using a carrier-bat?"

"Yes," replies Frankie, "But we didn't have much choice."

"Right," says Crawfield, looking down at the paper again. "You entered an unsanctioned doorway with an expired passport. Well, let's get this sorted then. Do you have Form DPS-13 filled out?"

At their blank faces, Crawfield smiles tightly. "Well, let's get DPS-13 filled out first." He points to the second stack of papers on his desk, inviting them to take a blank application. "You can only use green ink from a creature of the Dark, preferably a Hydra, given that it was extracted from the seventh head. Do you have an appropriate pen with you?"

Their blank faces answer him again. "Well. No mind, you may use one of mine." He gestures toward the coffee mug. "Will you be filling out an application, as well?" he asks Beau.

Beau looks over at Frankie. She has already started her application, leaning forward and resting her arm on the desk as she fills in the form with quick, deliberate pen strokes. She offers no advice but does raise her eyebrow, a minute expression change that might as well be an exaggerated shrug. He picks up a copy of Form DPS-13 and selects a pen from the coffee mug.

Crawfield watches them fill out their applications. "We'll just need a thumbprint, there," he interrupts, motioning to an ink pad that has suddenly appeared on the desk. When Beau begins the second page, Crawfield makes a tutting sound. "Sorry, I see you put your mother's married name. The form is asking for her maiden name. No worry, it happens all the time." Crawfield gives Beau another application. "I'll just incinerate this one, shall I?"

The chair squeaks as Crawfield swivels around. There is a marble pedestal behind his desk with a brass rod rising from its center. He clips the paper to the end of the rod and taps on the surface of the pedestal. The top slides back, and a palm-size dragon (an Inferior Flametongue from the looks of it, thinks Frankie, taking note of her small size and the characteristic horn on her snout) arises. Her leathery wings gently displace the air, ruffling the piece of paper above her. Her purple scales shimmer in the lighting overhead.

With a deep intake of breath, the dragon releases a stream of fire aimed at the application. The paper whooshes up into flames and the still-smoldering remains float down to rest on the dragon's head. She shakes them loose.

Crawfield smiles, thanking the dragon for her assistance by feeding her one of the dead flies he collects in a little jar by his typewriter. The dragon returns to her lair inside the pedestal, and Crawfield swivels back to Frankie and Beau.

He folds his hands together and continues their appointment. "I am also obligated to let you know about the fee schedule. The only acceptable form of payment is Time. You will have to make a withdrawal from your remaining balance on Earth." He pauses, looking at them expectantly.

"We're willing to make a withdrawal," says Frankie.

Beau nods.

"Right." Crawfield stamps their applications and then motions toward a room adjacent to his desk. "That'll be three hours and twenty-four minutes, to be paid in Real Time."

Clutching their receipts, they make their way toward the waiting room. As they step over the threshold, the timer above the door changes from 00:00 to 03:24 and begins its countdown.

CHAPTER 2

THE NEXT STEP

"This isn't right. There's been a mistake," says Penelope Church, clutching the spiral-bound booklet to her chest.

"I'm sorry, ma'am. But it's all explained in your welcome packet." The woman behind the desk barely looks up from her screen as she says this. Her long, pointed fingernails clack away on the keyboard. When she does look up, her green skin shimmers in the artificial glow lights bobbing above her head. She is not moved by the prickle of tears in Penelope's eyes, nor does she seem concerned about the red, splotchy hives that adorn her neck.

Penelope blinks back the tears once, twice, but then they flow. She can feel her skin getting warmer and redder, like it always does when she cries, and she takes a shaky breath. "I'm not supposed to be here," she says again, but the words get lost in her throat. She can hear her mother's voice in her head, admonishing her for crying in public. *Really, Penelope, there's no use in crying. You'll only make your mascara run.*

In the midst of the fear and worry about finding herself suddenly not-alive, Penelope feels a splinter of gratefulness at the thought that, perhaps, she might never have to hear that voice in person again—that her compendium of mother-isms repeating constantly in her head will begin to wither away in the face of starvation.

But then the coldness of Death, the buzzing globes of lights (which are surely highlighting the dark circles under her eyes), and the green-skinned, pointy-eared woman staring impassively at her bring the lump back to her throat. Her chest hurts with held-in tears, and so she lets them flow even more, her face crumpled and shiny.

An image of her mother, with perfectly coiffed hair, French manicured nails, and perfume that smells of flowers and money, rises annoyingly from her self-consciousness, to remind her that self-pity is not an attractive look on her.

Penelope sniffs loudly and straightens her shoulders, taking note of the name plaque on the desk. Wiping the tears from her cheeks, she says, "Johnsoniela, I would like to speak to your supervisor."

Penelope is always quite embarrassed when her mother says this, and yet, despite the audacity of the action, it has never failed. And indeed, the approach is once again proven effective when Johnsoniela shrugs and picks up the phone, wagging her fingers dismissively toward the low-backed bench to the left of the desk.

Penelope sits down on the very edge of the bench (blue with a clear plastic covering; tacky but sensible) and crosses her legs primly. While trying not to eavesdrop on Johnsoniela's conversation, she looks around the office, noting the dark wood-paneled walls with gilt-framed inspirational posters and the plush crimson carpet that makes her feel like she is walking on air.

Opposite the desk, there is a large window, and something like sunlight filters in through the tree outside. There is nothing beyond the tree branches, just a pale blue expanse. The angle of the branches makes her uncomfortable, and it takes her a few seconds to realize why: they stretch forward into the sky and not sideways or toward her.

She wonders if they are actually inside the tree. She hadn't seen the way in, after all, as she stood on the deck of a ferry, amidst a crowd of nameless faces and malformed figures, and tried very hard to prevent the panic attack rising in her chest. When they arrived, they were shuffled forward by a stern-faced attendant, and it was all Penelope could do to take a step forward without falling against the back of the large, purple-skinned person in front of her.

She tries to remember what happened before she found herself on a boat in the middle of the stars and the inky black river that had borne her, and so many others, to this strange, cold office. She remembers the cocktail that Beau made her after dinner when they went back to his house. His parents were away, and he raided his dad's liquor cabinet, producing a questionably dusty bottle of vodka. It tasted funny, but she drank it, feeling the fire of it burning against her sternum as she swallowed.

Perhaps he drugged her, and this is all a hallucination? No, drugs aren't really Beau's style, she thinks.

Maybe she choked on a canapé? Did they have canapés with their drinks? She shivers, for once, from uncertainty and not from the temperature in the room. She hates not remembering what happened. Penelope has an impeccable memory, but the minutes leading up to her death are absent. She brings her hand to her necklace and twists the chain around her fingers until they are tangled, then untangled and tangled again.

Regardless of how her death occurred, Beau must be devastated. She imagines him leaning over her lifeless body, his tears splashing onto her pale cheeks. He won't know how to go on without her. He'll spiral, falling into a life of addiction or something equally life-ruining, like bird watching. Her death will condemn Beau to a life of mediocrity.

She has to get home.

There is a clock on the wall, but there are no numbers and no hands to denote the passage of time. Just a soft ticking sound, barely loud enough to let her know she is still here and present, even if that present is in Death. To distract herself from the obscurity of time, she flips through her welcome packet, reading snippets here and there.

Welcome to the Next Step.

You may be dead, but you don't have to stop living. Here at the Next Step Office (Room 100), we appreciate our past while looking forward to the future.

Over the next few weeks, you may get flash-backs to your timely or untimely demise. Don't panic. This is completely normal and to be expected.

At the end of orientation, you will be given a few options for moving forward. First...

She tosses the packet down on the bench, annoyed by its very presence. The squeak of rubber-soled shoes draws Penelope's attention back to the office. Johnsoniela motions toward Penelope. "This is her."

Johnsoniela's supervisor introduces himself as Maxwell Fergus—Mr. Fergus—and he gives Penelope a wan smile before folding his hands together in front of his chest. His attire is tidy, a simple wool suit in a pleasing shade of brown, and his hair is brushed back neatly. He smiles tightly, showing a row of white, even teeth. She dislikes him immensely, even before he asks, "How can I help you?" with barely concealed boredom.

"Thank you for taking the time to see me," she says. "I know you must be busy. There's been a mistake, and I'm not supposed to be here. I want to go home."

Mr. Fergus gives her a gentle smile rife with condescension. "I see. I'm sorry you feel that way, Miss Church. I assure you that we take accusations such as this incredibly seriously, but our system for determining new arrivals is, quite frankly, foolproof."

"Well, I regret to inform you that you are wrong. And I would like to speak to your supervisor." Her voice is a high-pitched whine that hurts even her own ears, but she can't seem to control her volume. Her throat is tight with emotion. She hides an incoming hiccup by crossing her arms over her chest and settling her features into as stern a pout as she can muster.

"Miss Church—" he begins, but his voice falters against the tears gathering in her eyes and when he continues, his expression shifts into a distinct shade of discomfort at her emotional display. "Miss Church, I regret to inform you that there is nothing that can be done. Now, I understand that this can be a rough transition. I can provide you with some literature regarding our counseling services if you'd like."

"No, I would not like that, thank you."

Penelope suddenly feels annoyingly young. She is monumentally insignificant compared to Mr. Fergus's sneer. But the cold of Death has not yet sunk into her limbs, let alone her soul. She shouldn't be here, she reminds herself. She knows this is a mistake. A clerical error. A case of mistaken identity. It doesn't matter what the reason is; she feels the truth in her heart.

She takes a shaky breath, more out of habit than necessity, and exhales roughly, eyes closed as she straightens her spine and places her hands on her hips. Her mother's voice resounds in her head: *You can do this, Penelope Marie Church. You will do this.*

She opens her eyes to a darkened room, as if a cloud has just passed by the window. She thinks little of it as she wipes deftly at the tears still in the corners of her eyes.

Equally she pays little attention to the crackle of energy that gathers at her fingertips, sparking against the fabric of her dress and fizzling down her body, crashing against the wood floor. She takes a step closer to Mr. Fergus, her body oddly numb, her focus so narrow she doesn't notice the ground vibrating beneath her wedge heels. The walls seem to bend inward, creaking like a ship caught in a storm.

Mr. Fergus takes a step backward, reaching blindly for the door frame, huddling against it like a raft in rough waters.

"If you can't help me," she says stiffly, as a crack of lightning strikes the tree branch outside the window, "then find someone who can."

He swallows thickly, eyes flitting from Penelope to Johnsoniela and then back to Penelope. "Yes, of course," he says, the words sticking to the back of his throat, "I'll be right back."

She's sure he means to walk away with some measure of poise, but the action falls decidedly on the scampering side of ways to leave a room. Penelope chances a glance at Johnsoniela, who hurriedly redirects her gaze back to her computer screen. The clock ticks twenty-two times before Penelope hears footsteps coming down the hall again, and Mr. Fergus returns, his hands clasped in front of him. "If you'll come with me..."

She follows Mr. Fergus and they leave the office, taking an immediate turn to the right to continue down the hallway. She mentally catalogs the path, beginning to form a mental map of the office should she need to know the way back. (*Never rely on men for directions; you are more than capable of remembering the way, Penelope*).

The more they walk, the more she thinks they must be inside a large, hollowed-out tree. The walls are smooth, polished wood that flows down to the floors. The floors were originally wood as well—a completely round solid tunnel until linoleum was added. Penelope can see the edges of the tiles peeling up where floor becomes wall.

Mr. Fergus notices her gaze. "An attempt to modernize."

She thinks it looks cheap, and, considering Mr. Fergus's tone, he would agree. She wonders how the tree was hollowed out and imagines a large worm chomping away at the wood until it becomes pulp and sawdust. Is the worm still here, wandering the halls? If she gets lost, will the worm swallow her up? She suppresses a shiver and hugs her arms around her torso. When she selected her outfit for the night—a red sleeveless dress that tucks in tightly at her waist and hits just below her knees—it was with a balmy summer evening in mind.

Not...*this*.

"I'm sorry about the temperature," says Mr. Fergus. "It will take some time to get used to, I'm afraid."

"I won't have the time to get used to it," she insists. "I'll be leaving soon."

Mr. Fergus merely raises an eyebrow, his earlier fear seemingly forgotten with each step farther into the heartwood of the tree. They pass several other rooms, each with their own style of entryway.

There is a bright blue door marked "Room 146: Housing Services - we accept walk-ins!" and down from that is a rusty metal door labeled "Room 189: Torture Assignments - we accept walk-ins!"

The elevator is located at the end of the hallway, and Penelope watches her watery reflection in the stained-glass doors as they approach. She hesitates on the threshold, but Mr. Fergus motions for her to continue forward.

"The trip should only take a few seconds," he assures her, mistaking her reticence for fear of enclosed spaces. Really, it's that she feels a bit nervous not knowing exactly where they are heading. She's trying to leave this place, after all, not make her way farther in.

Mr. Fergus punches a button on the brass panel affixed to the wall and the elevator begins its ascent with a judder.

"How far up are we going?" She holds her torso tighter and focuses on the shadows of the floors as they move upward, shapes of the people beyond tinted blue, olive, and pale gold as she and Mr. Fergus travel from the first floor to the second and beyond. She instinctively counts the floors as they pass, losing her focus as the elevator gains speed.

"All the way to the top," says Mr. Fergus, eyes trained on the brass panel. There are rows of unlabeled red light bulbs, activating quickly as they pass the corresponding floor. There are too many red lights to count individually, but she estimates that there are at least five hundred floors in this tree—maybe more if one considers that not all of them may be accessible from this elevator. Crowning the rows of red is one white bulb framed in a brass star. It reminds Penelope of a Christmas tree.

"Are we going to...Heaven?"

He chuckles smugly and leans back on his heels, hands in his pockets. Mr. Fergus has regained the upper hand, and he is clearly capitalizing on it. "There is only one afterlife, and that's Death."

"Are we going to meet God? Or the Devil? Are they even real?"

"Probably. But they're not in charge around here."

"So, who is?"

"You'll find out soon enough," he mumbles. "Ah, here we are. The top."

The white star light flickers on and the doors open with a ding. He motions for her to exit first. To her left is a railing overlooking a large atrium, and she leans over to catch a glimpse. The metal of the railing is cold against her palm.

Below her is the bustling hub of the top floor. At first, the scene is mundane: the frantic energy of people heading to work, rushing to meetings, gulping coffee along the way, or waving to coworkers before rushing to catch an elevator.

But amid the activity, Penelope glimpses the occasional pointy ear, tail, or winged back that belies their current location. She sees green-skinned fae and reddish imps. She sees tall men with single eyes and very small creatures that zip about like fireflies. She sees combinations of half-human, half-beasts rushing to their next appointments, while animals walk upright and wear ties.

She follows Mr. Fergus down the ramp, descending into the atrium. Penelope sticks close to him, though she doesn't give in to her instinct to grab onto the back of his shirt. Their path briefly crosses with a mustachioed cat walking on two legs and his companion, a cloven-footed man.

"Look," she hears the cat saying, "Days of the week are artificial, human constructs that don't apply to thaumaturgic dimensions that exist outside of space and time, and Mondays should be illegal, don't you think?"

The cloven-footed companion opens his mouth to respond, but the answer is snatched away from

Penelope's ears as their paths uncross. Penelope and Mr. Fergus make their way toward a desk in the middle of the cavernous space, dodging fish-tailed employees in wheeled water tanks and see-through apparitions floating to important meetings.

"We're here to see Mr. Montague and Mr. Capulet," he says to the administrative assistant, a large tawny owl that blinks twice at them before pecking at the switchboard on her desk. Then, to Penelope, he adds, "Shakespeare has made quite a splash here recently, with his new play, *Macbeth III: Duncan's Revenge*. However, our current managers are quite the fans of his original works."

The administrative assistant hoots three times. With a pop, a door appears next to the desk, so suddenly that a few people walking by are forced to pivot, bumping into others with a murmur of annoyance.

"After you," says Mr. Fergus.

Penelope grips the handle and pushes the door inward.

CHAPTER 3

HORRIBLY AWRY

"How much longer?" asks Beau. He is slumped across a row of chairs, staring at the ceiling. Frankie is similarly slumped, though she has pulled a chair into the middle of the room, her feet propped up next to his. Together, they form a right angle.

Her eyes are closed, head bent awkwardly to the side, though he's sure she isn't sleeping. The coat she wears swallows her whole, but if he watches closely, he can see her shoulders rise and fall with her breath. There is a softness to her features that he hasn't seen since they were children. She's always worn her hair short, almost boyishly, but she's recently let it grow out, and it drapes across her shoulder, messy and tangled. He has the urge to brush it away, press his thumb against the smooth column of her neck so he can feel her pulse. Instead, he fidgets with the pack of cigarettes in his pocket.

In repose, wearing a too-large coat, her forehead relaxed, and her eyes closed, Frankie Hart doesn't look so scary.

He feels a swelling of emotion in his chest, a gratefulness he knows he will never be able to articulate. He's not foolish; he knows Frankie has her own reasons to help him, not the least of which is his bank account. He basically offered her a blank check in exchange for her services.

But, even with such incentive, she didn't have to help him. She didn't have to interrupt her Saturday night because Beau Astor made a mistake. She was well within her rights to refuse him. He half expected her to do just that when he sat down at the table. She scowled up at him, cheeks red and eyes narrowed at his impertinence. His mother would have scolded him for sitting down uninvited, for imposing his presence on someone—a young woman, no less—who so clearly did not want it.

His father would have scolded him, too, only it would have been because of Frankie's lack of familial wealth and social clout; politeness wouldn't have factored into it.

Beau wasn't thinking of his parents when he approached Frankie, however. He was thinking of the tattered remains of their friendship. He was thinking about the girl he knew before the churlish need to tease her arose, before the embarrassment that his grades were not quite as good or his jokes were not quite as funny took hold in the back of his mind, voiced by a rough timbre that sounded eerily similar to his father's.

He was thinking that some bonds transcend poor choices. He was hoping that some friendships remain, even if they sit forgotten on a shelf, collecting dust and grime until they're discovered one day in a fit of spring cleaning.

He thinks warmly of the summer before eighth grade. He doesn't remember how he and Frankie toiled away all eighty-four days of summer break, but he does remember that it contained hours at the arcade, wasting quarters on a game neither of them would win.

He remembers ice cream cones on the pier, their feet dangling over the edge, as they talked about comic books. He remembers a few scraped knees and at least one unfortunate bike crash involving Mrs. Howell's mailbox.

He tries to remember when it all went sideways. Was it when he suddenly got taller than her? When his hair darkened and girls started to smile shyly at him with cherry-glossed lips?

Maybe it was after the carnival on the board-walk when he won a goldfish, and he said he wanted Frankie to have it, knowing his father would sooner chuck it into the toilet before he let his son waste his time on such an insignificant creature. Frankie leaned up on her toes and gave him a kiss that tasted of cotton candy. His lips felt sticky, his stomach queasy, and his palms suddenly so sweaty that he almost dropped the plastic bag with the goldfish. The goldfish continued swimming in bored circles, and Beau suddenly developed a craving for cotton candy.

Perhaps it was when his father gave him the Talk?

That is, the Talk about responsibility and how to manage his own money (Beau learned about sex as all Astors learn about sex: in school, from a qualified healthcare professional, and from a fair bit of hands-on learning).

This reminds him of Penelope and her sudden death. He knew they were going to sleep together from the moment he held the car door open for her. He confirmed it at dinner when her hand strayed to his thigh, and she laughed too loudly at his jokes. When they made their way back to his house, she smiled slyly at him as he nonchalantly mentioned that his parents weren't home, and she eagerly accepted the invitation for after dinner drinks.

This date has gone horribly awry, he thinks. His whole *life* has gone horribly awry, he amends.

"Why are you staring at me?" asks Frankie.

Startled by her sudden alertness, he jumps slightly before crossing his arms with an awkward, affected casualness. "I was just wondering if you still have a scar on your elbow? The one from Mrs. Howell's mailbox?"

"You mean the scar I got after you dared me to ride with no hands, even though you knew that I would crash?"

"I didn't know—"

"No. We have spells for that. I got rid of it years ago." She sits up and stretches, looking over at the clock, a faceless circle with a soft ticking sound coming from its insides. "I reckon we've been in here long enough." She glances at Beau. "I'm going to check."

As Frankie opens the door and leans out to peer

at the countdown, Beau stands up to stretch the stiffness from his shoulders. He looks hopeful as she ducks back inside the room, but she just scowls.

"We still have another two hours." With a har-rumph, she throws herself into a seat.

Beau sits next to her and lets his head fall back until it rests on the wood-paneled wall with a soft thud. "What if we just left? Would anyone even notice?"

Frankie leans her head against the wall as well, folding her arms. The coat bunches up around her neck, the stiff collar pressing against her cheek. "Trust me, I want to get moving again too, but it's too risky. They'll be paying attention to me now."

There is a beat of silence.

The ticking of the faceless clock fills the space.

"So, you're a Reaper-in-Training?"

"Yep."

Tick, tock. Tick....

"What does that entail?"

"Quite a few hours of training."

Tick, tock.

"And then?"

"Well, then I'll be certified," she says plainly.

"Do you have to take, like, a test or something?"

"No." There is a moment of silence, and he looks at Frankie, whose own gaze is resolutely aimed at a spot on the opposite wall. "There's a...sacrifice," she adds eventually, in a small voice.

"Like, you have to sacrifice something?"

"Sort of." She sighs and hugs her arms tighter to her chest. "A sacrifice of me. I'll be the sacrifice."

"You're going to die?" he asks breathlessly; the realization squeezes his lungs just as her curse did in ninth grade.

"That's one way to look at it."

"What's the other way?"

"Certification." She sucks in a deep breath and shifts in her seat, bringing her knees up to her chest. "Please stop asking about this."

"Did you choose this?"

She gives him a sideways look. "It's tradition."

He swallows and then says, with a worried line in between his eyebrows, "Your family chose this for you."

He had intended it to be a question, but it comes out as a statement, a truth that draws him closer to her.

He knows the feeling of having dreams stymied by family obligations. Except in his case, it's all very banal: a rich family expecting their only son and heir to follow the family path of ivy-league schools and a law degree. But Frankie's family will be the death of her. She is already gone; her fate is sealed. He hates them for taking her away. "That's messed up."

She shrugs, the movement jagged but well-practiced, and says, "All families are psychotic in their own ways."

"Mine wants me to become a lawyer."

"You mean they care about your future and want you to succeed in life?" she says with a short, humorless laugh. "How awful!"

He grunts at her sarcasm but smirks. "I know. I'm a terrible cliché."

She lifts a shoulder. "Isn't everybody?"

"Frankie..." He reaches out, and her eyes widen with the realization of his intention, even though he isn't entirely aware of it himself. Then again, Frankie could always read his thoughts, even before he thought them. His mind conjures a wild, feverish image that must be writ large on his face, perhaps even projected against his pupils like a movie screen: him leaning in to press his lips against hers.

He could do it, so easily. They are so close to each other.

Her mouth parts, just slightly. He thinks of the last time her lips touched his—a too-sticky meeting of mouths that still makes his cheeks burn with regret that he was too young to know what to do next. He stopped talking to her soon after that. Does she still taste like cotton candy?

But then a tear escapes her eye, and, instead of leaning closer, he touches his thumb to her cheek, wiping it away. "I'll still be able to see you. Right?"

"Yes." She turns away from him. "Don't be silly. You can't get rid of me that easily. We have a contract. I'll haunt you until the day you die." She laughs gently. "Besides, you'll have a passport to Death, soon. You'll be able to come and go as you please."

CHAPTER 4

A RELATED INCIDENT

Two text-based documents. This is the sum of Penelope's life.

"It's the sum of most people's lives, to be honest," says Mr. Fergus.

He gives Mr. Montague and Mr. Capulet a sidelong look. They continue their chess game in silent contemplation, just as they have been doing for millennia, as Mr. Fergus explained when they first walked in. He loudly voiced his disappointment in their lack of surprise, adding quietly to Penelope that he was hoping their intrusion would have at least paused the game for a few minutes.

But alas, Penelope Church walked in with her perfect posture and her disgruntled expression, and Mr. Montague merely waved his hand at the dusty computer terminal in the corner.

It took some fiddling with the search options to find the right Penelope Church, and now there she is: two text-based documents and a slideshow.

"What's that?" she asks, leaning over Mr. Fergus's shoulder. She points to a paperclip icon. "There's an attachment."

He clicks on the link. "It's a related incident. Something pertinent to your death."

At first, the related incident seems to be another case file. It begins with some personal identifiable information and a brief bio, followed by an incident report and timeline breakdown. As they read, Penelope's anger grows, heat rising up from her chest, coloring her cheeks and making her fingers tingle.

"Do you know this...uh, Francesca Hart?" Mr. Fergus asks.

"No. I mean, yes. Barely. We go to the same school. She lives a few doors down from my boyfriend." Penelope straightens and takes a deep breath, stretching her fingers against the anxiety traveling up her arms. "I don't get it. We barely speak to each other. What happened?"

"Well," Mr. Fergus says as he clicks the scroll bar. "It seems that Francesca Hart is a witch. A Reaper-in-Training, technically. She was doing a bit of spell work, nothing crazy. A grounding ritual." A few more clicks. "Ah, but her protection circle failed. It's a small thing, really, but she must have had some anger pent up or maybe you were merely just close by. It—" He swallows and turns to look at her. "Your timeline file was corrupted; the root directory's been altered. This is a clerical error. I must apologize, Miss Church. This wasn't supposed to happen to you."

"Well, obviously," she says. "It's what I've been trying to tell you since I arrived here. I want to go home now."

He closes the file and turns off the computer. The screen goes black with a zap, extinguished just like the tiny flare of hope in Penelope's chest. She knows what he's going to say before he even opens his mouth.

"Miss Church, there's no way to restore you back to Life. Death is a one-way ticket."

Penelope can feel her eyes getting watery, and her breath becoming thin and short. The tingling in her fingers gets worse, traveling up her arms and to her lips. Her mother's voice admonishes her: *You will not start crying. I forbid it.*

"That is unacceptable," she says quietly, though she isn't sure if it's her that's talking or the figment of her mother, which seems to echo in her head with an infinite scowl.

The coldness of Death has started its descent into her limbs, as electric blue energy crackles around her fingers. She looks over at the two immortal beings who are so revered by the people here, though she cannot fathom why.

It's just two men frowning at a chessboard. She hasn't seen either of them make a move yet.

She's always been good at games and at solving puzzles. There is satisfaction in working through a problem and finding the solutions, applying different scenarios to find the one that makes the equation complete.

Her grandfather taught her how to play chess when she was seven, but she hasn't played a full game since he passed away. Thoughts of chess are never far from her mind, though. Her mother considers it a waste of energy. *It's childish*. Penelope once tried to share her love of the game with Beau, but he was terrible at it. At the time, he suggested she join the Chess Club because he could see how much she enjoyed it. She balked at him. She does have her limitations.

Penelope moves closer to the chessboard, surveying the current arrangement of pieces. She makes a few imaginary moves, running through the variable consequences in her head until she's confident that she's found the most efficient and effective solution.

She reaches for Mr. Capulet's white queen and moves it to the D8 square, checking Mr. Montague. She takes Mr. Capulet's queen with Mr. Montague's rook on H8. Then, Penelope brings Mr. Capulet's rook home from D1 to D8, trapping Mr. Montague's king on the back rank behind a phalanx of pawns.

"Checkmate," she says, as two sets of fuzzy, blinking eyes look up at her. "Now, which one of you is going to fix this for me?"

"How could you ask me that?"

For a moment, Beau is worried he's offended her. "I'm sorry, I just—"

"I'm joking." She bumps his arm with her elbow, and he wonders if she is actually leaning closer to him or if the nothing-clock ticking is making his head go a bit funny. "And anyway, I don't know how it'll happen. That's up to my grandmother to decide."

"I think I would want to die fighting."

She rolls her eyes. "It'll most likely be poison. That's usually how we do it."

"Hey, Frankie," he says suddenly, his voice rough with emotion. "I'm sorry for all the mean things I've said about you. I didn't mean them, not really."

She turns to him, her eyes narrowing. "So, if you don't think my glasses make me look like a frog, why did you say it? And don't give me some non-sense about how you've always liked me, but you didn't know how to show it. Boys are not as emo-tionally stunted as the media leads us to believe."

He shakes his head and turns in his chair, reaching for her arm, as if his words will be made stronger by physical contact. "I missed you, that's all. I missed having you as a friend. I was angry that we stopped talking. I was angry about a lot of things that had nothing to do with you. I lashed out."

He is overwhelmed with uncertainty. With fear. With gratitude. With longing. He feels them all like equal slices of his heart. He tries to remind himself of Penelope's lips, the way she places a hand on his arm when she's talking to him, and the way she looks up at him through her eyelashes and presses her thigh against his. He tries to remember that he loves Penelope, and he's planning on asking his mother for his grandmother's ring any day now.

He tries, and yet he forgets.

The chill of the room has sunk into his bones, despite the heavy coat he wears. He wonders what it would be like to be here, in this room, for an eternity. Lifetimes spent with Frankie, waiting around but doing so much more than that—waiting around, yes, but talking, laughing, and dreaming.

He thinks of Penelope and the last conversation they had. He thinks of her certainty that they will be married one day. She takes comfort in the assumption that they will live happily ever after. She's made no secret of the fact that she expects to build a future with Beau.

The future isn't here, though. The ticking of the clock is hollow, meaningless without arms to count the seconds.

What is here is this:

Frankie.

The overwhelming breadth of loss when their friendship ended.

The twisting feeling in his gut as he thinks of those silent moments on the pier with her, the moments his chest felt open and his laugh as bright as the summer sun.

Everything between then and now feels like a dream. How long have they been in this room? He feels a bit mad, a bit off-kilter. Who knew Death could make him feel more alive than he's felt in years?

He parts his lips as he touches her cheek the same way he had earlier. But this isn't the same, and he can feel it.

She can feel it too.

"Beau, don't."

His face is close to hers. He can see her freckles and a small scar right below her eye. She presses her hand against his chest, gathering his shirt in between her fingers. He can't tell if it's to pull him closer or push him away.

Maybe both.

He thinks of her imminent death and how indignant he felt on her behalf. She grew up knowing her role in her family and has long since accepted her fate. Beau hasn't had the luxury of time to come to terms with the fact that Frankie's life will end at eighteen. Only a few months away, if he remembers correctly.

What if they had more time? What if he hadn't squandered away that precious slice of life with his own insecurities? What if—?

"What about Penelope?" she whispers. Their faces are so close, her words brush against his lips.

"I think accidentally killing her might put a damper on the relationship," he whispers back, tasting cotton candy and sea salt. Is that the ocean roaring in his ears or is it just his heartbeat? "I think that means we've broken up."

Slowly, she leans back, pulling her hand away from his chest. "We're here to find her. We shouldn't lose focus."

The ticking of the clock fills the space between them.

The hallway to Room 349 is dreary and damp. Penelope almost misses the shimmering energy of the top floor because here, on the third floor, the energy is heavy, an oppressive weight of time lost to the peculiarities of a formal document.

Plus, the buzzy glow lights have made their triumphant return, and Penelope wipes at her cheeks, wishing she had thought to slip a compact mirror into her pocket before she died.

"Explain this to me again," she says to Mr.

Fergus as he leads her down the hallway, past Room 310: Identity Crisis Prevention and Rooms 323-348: Tax Office.

"We will be giving you a special issuance passport. While some of our residents are eligible for passports, almost all of them have certain limitations on where they can visit and for how long. Due to your unique circumstances, our Esteemed Managers agree that you should be eligible for the maximum time of travel allowed. That is—" He pauses outside of Room 349, the pebbled glass of the door revealing nothing of its inhabitants, "—one month. You will be able to travel into Life for one month at a time. At the end of the month, you must return here, to Death, to get your passport stamped and your visa renewed for another month."

Penelope opens her mouth, but Mr. Fergus is already speaking again. "I know this isn't ideal, Miss Church. And I sincerely apologize."

"Thank you." She smiles softly. "I appreciate your honesty and your assistance."

Mr. Fergus blushes as he watches Penelope Church turn swiftly on her heel and push open the door.

He clears his throat, trying to dislodge a dreadful feeling that has been growing steadily since Miss Church waltzed into his afterlife. Maxwell Fergus is often considered an optimist—a cauldron-half-full kind of man—but even he felt Penelope's bravado was futile.

And yet, she succeeded where so many others have failed. Her ability to manipulate Death is astounding, and quite frankly, terrifying. The lightning. The sparks of energy. The way the walls leaned in.

His sense of self-preservation kicked in quite quickly, and he escalated her issue right up to the tippy-top of the organization chart, something he hasn't done in at least a millenia.

For a moment, he tries to fool himself into believing that it is merely that sense of self-preservation that led him to help her. But who is he kidding? This choked feeling against his sternum is empathy. He's sure of it.

It feels like something has died in his chest.

He utterly hates it.

"All done!" says Crawfield.

Frankie pulls her coat tighter around herself as she exits the room, with Beau following right behind her. He can still feel where her hand touched his chest—five burning tendrils of memory that connect him to her—and he rubs his chest in an unconscious attempt to keep the feeling from dissipating.

He's sad to leave the waiting room and return to the crushing dreariness of the Passport Services office; a yawn is already forming at the back of his throat. But the room they enter is different, as if, in the three hours and twenty-four minutes they've been gone, the space, the desks, and the employees have been uprooted, replaced by an entirely different office providing an entirely different service. The energy is palpable. Beau's yawn is immediately forgotten.

"What's going on?" he asks, looking at an excited group gathered around a desk in the corner.

"Oh, that," answers Crawfield, "is for a special issuance passport. And of course, I was already mid-appointment when the application came in, meaning *Barbara* gets to execute it."

"I've never heard of a special issuance passport," says Frankie.

Crawfield scoffs. "Of course not, they don't just hand them out. But some girl got herself accidentally killed and complained so much, they decided to make an exception."

Frankie begins walking toward the group before Crawfield even finishes speaking. She elbows her way to the center, with Beau only a few steps behind. He reaches for her, worried that the group will swallow her up, but she's too quick, her hand slipping from his instantly, as a tall purple-skinned passport agent fills the space in front of him. He politely squeezes past, bumping into a mermaid in a wheeled tank

He hears Penelope's voice ringing out above the crowd. "You! Get away from me!"

He elbows past a yellow-eyed woman with a snake familiar draped around her neck. The snake hisses briefly, assesses Beau as a non-threat, and then returns to the excitement in the middle of the crowd. Squeezing in between a large crow wearing a monocle and a powdery-skinned vampire with long, graying hair, Beau finally finds himself at the front.

With mouths agape and eyes darting between the two young humans excitedly, the crowd watches as Penelope, an inch taller than Frankie due to her choice in footwear, leans forward, expertly aiming a scathing expression at the source of her ire, Frankie.

Penelope looks just as Beau last saw her.

Despite being dead, Penelope's makeup is flawless. Her dress is unwrinkled and hugs her tiny waist. Yet, he can't help but conjure up the memory of her sprawled on the floor, gasping for breath, her spilled drink staining her dress. The stain is still there, splashed across her torso. He wonders vaguely if they have dry cleaners in Death.

"That's no way to treat someone who came all this way to help you," Frankie is saying.

"I don't care if you're here to help me or not. You're the reason I'm here in the first place, Frankie Hart."

The words hit Frankie like a slap across her face. Her arms drop to her sides, and she frowns, giving Beau a lost look that makes his chest tighten.

"What do you mean? It was my fault," he says, taking a step closer.

Penelope looks at Beau for the first time, a smile brightening her features. She wrinkles her nose at the tattered army coat, plucking an invisible bit of fluff from the shoulder before flinging her arms around his neck.

"What are you doing here?" she asks.

"I came to get you. Frankie helped me get here and then—"

Her eyes harden, and she breaks away from Beau's embrace to face Frankie. "It was a stupid spell she was casting. Only she did it wrong and now I'm here."

Beau looks at Frankie, whose expression is caught somewhere between bewilderment and regret. Her glasses do make her look like a frog, though he wouldn't make the mistake of telling her again.

"All that matters is that I've found you," he says, giving Penelope a lopsided smirk that makes her lean closer to him. He feels a little guilty diffusing the tension with that smirk. He knew it would work, as it always does, but it somehow feels cheap to employ it in this situation, especially since he had been thinking about kissing Frankie only a few moments ago.

Penelope places a hand on his chest, and Beau can't help but recall that Frankie's hand had been there, in the same place, not even ten minutes ago. He glances up at Frankie, whose mouth is set in a firm line.

"And now we can go home," he adds, eyes darting back to Penelope for a moment before returning to Frankie. "Right?"

Frankie nods and looks away with a sniff.

CHAPTER 5

STYGIAN JEWEL

The *Stygian Jewel* glides smoothly through ink-black waters that reflect the stars above so clearly, Beau isn't sure where the sky ends, and the water begins.

The water, belonging to that of the infamous River Styx, will bring them out of Death and back into Life, as Frankie explained. "The Passport Office isn't the first step for most people. Actually, most people don't qualify for a passport. If we had died, we would have gone through a different entryway," she said, as they boarded the ferry.

In fact, there is only one known permanent

imperfection in the fabric of reality, and it serves as the main threshold between Life and Death. How the Imperfection occurred and how long it has existed is undocumented, but, as the centuries fly by, its presence remains. It acts as the primary point of entry for anyone passing between Life and Death. A fee is required to cross one of the rivers that spread out from the Imperfection and beyond, to what is often considered Death proper.

And yet, not everyone who passes from Life into Death travels along the River Styx, or any of the sister-rivers for that matter. Some are assigned a Reaper, who has the unique ability to circumnavigate this process by opening a door to most anywhere in Death. And of course, there are some who are unwilling or unable to pay their fare to continue on the correct path, causing a bit of a bottleneck at the Imperfection's threshold.

As people began to settle in, refusing to move forward for various reasons, Souls-Town-on-the-Styx was soon created, cobbled together from ramshackle wishes and regrets and other random accoutrement that seemed to appear out of thin air. Like most things going against the current, the current soon gave up, happily circling around the island in an aquatic roundabout and branching off at various points to once again form the five rivers of Death. Souls Town has since become a major hub that is unavoidable if one desires to go from Life into Death, or, in some extremely rare cases, Death into Life.

The Styx is the most direct route between Death proper and Souls Town, and so it is the most popular. The *Stygian Jewel* is just one of the vessels that sail the dark waters of the Styx, and it offers the most economical mode of transportation into Death proper.

Occupancy on the ferry is sparse today and the trio sit on the lower deck, on a hard wooden bench pockmarked from years of use. However, the *Stygian Jewel* is a pleasant enough vessel, with a small bar upstairs and an observation deck dotted with reclining chairs. The red-and-white striped awning whips in the breeze above them, yet the waters are calm and the ferry glides along with little disruption.

Despite these attributes, Beau still wonders why they can't exit the same way he and Frankie entered: through a magical door conjured by Frankie.

"We can't trust doors right now," Frankie says, but Beau has a feeling that it has more to do with the shaken look in Frankie's eyes when she realized that her magic had done something wrong. That it had escaped her control just long enough to lash out at the nearest living creature, like a car sliding on a slick wet road.

"I can't wait to get home," says Penelope, leaning against Beau. "I don't know if I'll ever feel warm again."

Probably not, he thinks. Still, he dutifully slips out of his jacket—Frankie's jacket, though he doesn't tell Penelope that—and places it gently around her shoulders. She kisses him on the cheek in gratitude.

"Maybe when we get back, we can try that cute Italian restaurant on Tenth Street?" she asks, hugging the coat tighter. It's an awful color on her, but he's at least smart enough not to comment on the fact. She may not be able to curse him like Frankie, but there are some punishments worse than boils or suffocation.

"That sounds great," he says enthusiastically, though he can feel the reluctance at the back of his throat. He wishes he had a cigarette; the smoke would feel more pleasant than this noxious half-truth.

But what is the full truth, he wonders. Is it that he no longer has feelings for Penelope? Somehow, this doesn't feel quite right either. He still holds a tender sort of affection for Penelope, an almost-love that could grow into something more if given the time, and he most certainly doesn't want to break her heart.

Yet, he can't deny his feelings for Frankie. It's like a river of fire coursing in his chest and, even now, he licks his lips, remembering how close they had been to Frankie's just a few hours ago.

No matter what the truth is, he refuses to lose Frankie again, and he wonders how long you should wait after someone dies before it's okay to break up with them?

Frankie would know, he thinks, looking over at the silent, brooding figure to his left. She always has an answer. He envies her for it.

Frankie is hunched over, her coat bunched up around her ears. He knows she has been crying, her eyes rimmed with redness. He's not sure what she's feeling, but he has a few guesses. Shame, regret, foolishness, and maybe something toward him? Something soft and yielding, like a moonflower, slowly unfolding for the night sky?

Something changed in that room.

They changed in that room.

"I'm going to get a drink from the bar upstairs.

Would you like to join me?" says Penelope.

"Yeah, sure. I'll be there in a few minutes."

Penelope narrows her eyes at him. "You're going to smoke a cigarette, aren't you?"

He gives her a smirk and lifts a shoulder in a silent *You got me*, as he reaches for his crumpled pack of cigarettes in his pocket. She rolls her eyes, almost affectionately despite the fact that smoking is one of his many habits that she despises.

When Penelope is out of sight, Beau turns back to Frankie, slipping the unsmoked cigarette back into his coat pocket. He nudges her boot with his own. "You okay?"

There is no answer. She might as well be among the stars twinkling above them. The space between them seems to be shifting, growing, changing. There is a gulf opening between them as Frankie stews further in her emotions.

So, he fills the silence. He talks, crafting long, winding sentences that don't quite go anywhere and posing questions he answers for himself. He starts with uplifting platitudes, expecting at least a snort at his "We all make mistakes," or maybe a long-suffering sigh when he says, "At least you updated your passport, so this won't happen again."

Frankie remains adrift, so he segues into the mundane, making useless observations about the weather ("It's pretty dark out here. I've never seen stars like this before") or jabbering away with pointless comments about school ("Mr. Singh said my essay was boorish. Can you believe that?").

He knows Penelope is waiting for him. He can feel her impatience like a physical beam of light, aimed in his direction despite the fact that he's not in her line of sight. He thinks of her waiting at the bar for him, alone, probably drumming her nails on the counter and pouting.

But, still, he fills the silence around Frankie, enveloping her in the mundane to bring her closer, back to the river stretching beyond them.

Back to him.

He feels quite frantic to do so. They have lost

so much time already, their friendship frayed by his immaturity and fear. He wants to make it right before they disembark.

He is telling her about a comic book he read last week when the coat unfurls, and Frankie sits up. She shifts out of the coat and rolls up the sleeve of her sweater. She angles her elbow so he can see the shiny, pink scar, courtesy of Mrs. Howell's flamingo-shaped mailbox and a dare.

"You still have it?" He runs a calloused finger across it. "Why did you tell me you didn't?"

"I could have gotten rid of it, but I didn't want to. It reminds me of you. And I didn't want to forget you. When I die, that is." She pushes her sleeve back down and, after a moment of thought, grabs his hand. "We can't change the past."

He nods. "Another time, another place..."

She shrugs.

The water laps gently against the boat, the smell of fish and sulfur mixing in the air. The salt from the water is already drying on their cheeks.

The coldness of Death begins to slink away, their limbs humming with warmth.

The silhouette of Souls-Town-on-the-Styx looms closer, a cluster of multi-colored lights, a rainbow amidst the black and gold of the Styx.

In the distance, a thick, shiny tentacle rises out of the depths, as if stretching after a long day's work, and then disappears so gently the water doesn't even ripple.

Frankie and Beau are still holding hands. He knows Penelope will begin to wonder what's taking him so long, that she might be tempted to come back down—and when she does, he knows he shouldn't be holding Frankie's hand, but he can't move.

Not yet. Not when the moonflower has just begun to twist open under the starlight. He wonders when he became so poetic. How's that for boorish, Mr. Singh?

So, he holds Frankie's hand, and he holds his breath, knowing this moment will break and trying to remember every second of it before it does.

Penelope sips her cocktail, appreciating the hint of absinthe and orange on her tongue. She's happy to note that although her body feels cold and oddly numb, her taste buds are still functional and the anise flavor lingers pleasantly on the inside of her cheeks.

There are so many things to learn about this new reality, but Penelope's mind wanders as she gazes absentmindedly out at the river. The view isn't so bad, if one can get used to the sheer monotony of it. Just stars and black water.

It could even be considered quite pretty, really, with the stars sparkling like diamonds against the stark contrast of the dark sky. She wonders if Souls Town is like that as well, darkness and luminescence sitting side-by-side. As Frankie describes it, it sounds dreary but she holds out hope that it's glitzy and metropolitan, and perhaps Frankie is just uncultured enough not to notice.

Regardless of her personal opinions, she knows this is a vista she would do well to acclimate to, seeing how she will be viewing it every month.

She imagines herself sitting here at the bar, sipping cocktails with her monogrammed luggage set she received for her birthday last year. She envisions herself passing through the glamorous Souls Town once every month to have her special—*important*—passport stamped.

She will wear her Chanel sunglasses and perhaps a scarf over her hair so she'll look particularly glamorous and mysterious. She will wear her favorite shade of red lipstick (Fire Vixen No. 2) and Beau will meet her at the dock to take her to their townhouse in New Haven, where he will attend classes at Yale and she will...

She cocks her head to the side, wondering how she will occupy her time. In Life, she had activities and obligations. Can you still have hobbies even if you're dead?

She decides that she will start her own personal

styling business. That's what she had intended to do when she was still alive, and she sees no reason to change her plans now.

Yes, she thinks, looking around the bar, noting the troll in an ill-fitting suit. Not only is he wearing the wrong size for his body type, but black is not the best color for him; he'd do better with a soft, warm brown and a double-breasted jacket.

She observes the pixie whose shift dress barely allows for her gossamer wings. She'd have far better movement and comfort if she went for an empire waistline and a longer skirt. At the very least, something sleeveless would highlight her wings, which are the loveliest shade of lavender.

Penelope takes another sip of her drink and smiles at the silhouette of Souls Town looming closer. Yes, she certainly has her work cut out for her, but luckily, Penelope Church loves a challenge.

"Why did you think you had killed her, anyway?" asks Frankie, softly, after a few moments of silence.

Like Beau, she knows this moment will fall apart. Any second now, he will go upstairs to continue his date with Penelope, leaving Frankie to ponder if she will ever feel his lips on hers.

No, not even that.

She would be left wondering where their friendship could have gone if left unfettered by life and her imminent death.

Souls-Town-on-the-Styx should be a comfort. That they have all come out of this relatively unscathed should be a relief. Frankie's contract with Beau will be complete and her payment received. It's why she agreed to this whole thing in the first place, after all—the money. It was purely selfish, she reminds herself, and then follows it up with a concerted effort to believe it.

And yet, she hates the sight of the island, looming closer to them.

Beau sighs, bringing her attention back to him

and their hands entwined and the question she had asked him. "I'm surprised you didn't ask earlier."

"Plausible deniability." She bumps his shoulder with her own. "So...?"

"I had a mango martini before we started making out."

"And?"

"She's allergic to mangoes."

CHAPTER 6

DEATH DAY PARTY

Frankie knew it was a risk to invite Beau to her Death Day Party. The family affair has rarely been witnessed by anyone outside of her family, though it certainly isn't unheard of for a significant other or friend to attend the party.

However, what is even rarer is for the event to be attended by someone without an ounce of mischief in their blood, which is a category into which Beau falls firmly. And yet, none of this supersedes the true rarity, which is that Frankie has such a person to even invite in the first place, mischief affiliated or otherwise.

Thankfully, Beau won't be allowed to see the actual death. Not even her parents will get to witness it. Her demise is hers, and hers alone. Until then, Frankie stands in the corner of the garden, a glass of champagne gripped tightly in her hand, waiting for Beau to arrive. Technically speaking, she is still underage and, yet it hardly seems reasonable to follow such rules when one is going to die in...Frankie glances at her watch. Two hours.

She takes a large gulp and considers how to best make her way from the corner of the garden to the drinks table without passing through the throng of her family members. They are ecstatic that she has passed her Reaper exams with distinction, and there seems to be no end to the handshakes, shoulder pats, and high-fives. She adjusts her beret and makes sure her black turtle-neck is tucked into her black jeans. She'll be able to change her outfit in Death, but, as a Reaper, she'll appear in Life as she died. She crafted her final outfit with that in mind, pairing her favorite articles of clothing with her most comfortable combat boots. She's even added a pair of silver studs to her ears.

Perhaps Beau won't even come, she thinks. Perhaps their time spent in Death did not overshadow his aversion to her, as she had led herself to believe. Perhaps the handholding, and the charged, fevered looks, and the almost-kiss did nothing to convince him to break up with Penelope.

Perhaps, like most things in life, it all meant nothing in the end.

This is when she sees him walk through the garden gate, a head taller than most of her family, curls sticking up as if he's just run his hand through them.

Her father glances at Beau curiously, and they exchange a few words. With a sigh, Frankie makes her way over to them.

"It's a bit unusual for Frankie to—well—" Her father stumbles over the words "—have friends."

This is, of course, not entirely true. Frankie has plenty of friends. However, what is true is that she is quite good at keeping people at arm's length. She has never had someone close enough to invite to a family function, which has so far suited her just fine, and in fact, she's not quite sure what brave initiative had risen in her chest when she invited Beau today. Surely, it was an unusual display of emotional vulnerability, with display being the operative word. The risk that he would decline, citing a previous obligation that would undoubtedly be too flimsy to be real, was high.

And yet, he agreed. Readily.

Happily.

The memory still sends a wave of warmth across her cheeks.

Despite his assurances that he absolutely wanted to be there and to see her, her nerves had not been assuaged until just now, as Beau smooths his face into something polite, all straight lines and slightly raised eyebrows. It's a practiced facade of manners, but Frankie doesn't miss the flicker of annoyance; her father's lack of confidence in her social skills has not gone unnoticed by Beau, and Frankie feels a little jolt of pleasure that he feels offended on her behalf.

"I'm honored, then," he says. "That she would deign to associate with me is a reflection of her good character more so than of mine."

Frankie raises an eyebrow, not bothering to hide her smirk. It is uncommon to see Beau displaying his Astor manners.

It's surprisingly charming.

Her father seems impressed, as well. "Let me introduce you to the family."

"I can do that," says Frankie.

Her father looks at her with a half-smile, as if he's just realized that his little girl is an adult. She wonders if he's sad that he won't get to see her become more than what she is right now.

Or perhaps he's simply proud that she is upholding family traditions with a considerable amount of aplomb. Frankie takes Beau's hand and pulls him away from her father.

"Well," says Frankie. "That was my dad. Jonathan. He's forty-six and dislikes peas."

She introduces Beau to her mother ("forty-seven, loves peas") and her grandmother ("unknown age, doesn't give a toss about peas, would sell her own soul for a bottle of whiskey").

"And this," says Frankie, her voice wavering for the first time since Beau arrived, "is my great-great-Aunt Francesca. The one I'm named after."

"And the one who has recently retired," says great-great-Aunt Francesca. Physically, she is the same age as Frankie, but there is something off about her coloring. She is far paler than she should be, particularly with the late-summer sun shining down on her face. She seems incongruous, her attire more reminiscent of the turn of the century than 1993. Her default expression is blandly interested, and she seems somehow removed from the conviviality of the party. Then again, great-great-Aunt Francesca is dead.

"Aunt Frank, I would like you to meet

my—friend, Beau Astor." Frankie, it would seem, has a little trouble saying the word as well.

"It's lovely to meet you," says Aunt Frank. She turns her head to the side and looks curiously at him. "You've been to Death."

He nods. "Yes, there was a...an incident. Frankie helped me sort it out. I have a passport now."

Aunt Frank frowns. "But you are alive. Frankie, you're not breaking regulations before you've even taken your post?"

"It's fine, Aunt Frank," says Frankie, her attention on her glass of champagne. "He signed a contract and everything. He won't tell anyone. Besides," Frankie looks up with a smirk, her eyes sliding to Beau. "I trust him with my life."

Aunt Frank isn't amused. "You know it's a great honor to be selected for this position. The Harts have a long-standing reputation of excellence in the Reaper community. We were hand-selected by Charon himself, centuries ago."

Frankie lets her smirk fall, though it maintains

an admirable attempt at an encore. "I understand, ma'am."

Aunt Frank nods. "See that you continue to do so."

"Yes, ma'am," she says, eyes trained on her scuffed boots. When Aunt Frank wanders away, Frankie adds, just under her breath. "I'm just dying to keep the family traditions intact."

Beau snorts, and Frankie smirks up at him before taking his hand and pulling him away. They round the corner of the house, as Frankie leads him to the swing on the back porch. She barely makes it around the corner before a bubble of laughter escapes, causing more than a few startled looks in their direction.

Beau smiles and squeezes her hand as his laughter joins her. She remembers the sound so well from her childhood, better than her own laugh. She spent many hours teasing it from his mouth, and a soft, warm bloom of emotion spreads through her chest at the sight and sound of Beau Astor so happy to be in her presence.

As the afternoon wanes, the back garden becomes considerably less crowded, the drinks table long depleted. Frankie manages to sneak the last bottle of champagne, and she and Beau sit among the rosebushes taking sips and ignoring the fact that she will be a ghost very soon.

She feels the back of his hand against hers, and, with an uncharacteristic spark of courage, she twists her wrist, so that they are palm-to-palm. Beau is the one who laces their fingers together, and she glances up at him.

"Almost time," she says quietly.

Beau's eyebrows crease together. "Explain it to me again."

She recites the words she's repeated to herself since she was old enough to talk. "Death will be swift. After I die, I'll open a doorway and walk through, which sort of affirms the whole death thing, like sealing an envelope. Then, I'll move into my dorm in the Reaper's Quarters."

"I'll see you soon, though. Right?"

"Yeah, of course. You've got your passport."

He nods, then seems to consider something, like he's tasting the words on his tongue before he lets them loose. His eyes flicker down to her lips. "I need to tell you—"

She kisses him.

It's the champagne, she thinks, but she knows it's not.

There is a split second where Frankie feels panic rising in the back of her mind at his lack of response. But then he shifts, moves so that their lips line up perfectly. She feels his hand on the back of her neck.

Her skin tingles with the reality of him.

It's a truth she didn't realize she needed: lips sliding against lips, hands hurting from clench-ing each other, the taste of champagne, and a bit of smoke from the cigarette he had just before he arrived.

"Sorry," she says. "It's the champagne—"

"Don't." He takes a shaky breath. "Don't blame the champagne. It's like saying you didn't mean it."

"I meant it," she says, and then, her voice hesitant and small, she adds, "Did you?"

"I definitely meant it." But even though she can feel the veracity in his words, his expression darkens.

She leans back.

"It's Penelope," he begins. "We haven't had a chance to really talk—"

"Oh," she says stiffly. She thinks about saying something scathing, but can't muster the jealousy.

Of course, he's still with Penelope. Even dead, Penelope is better suited for Beau than her. She's pretty, intelligent, and sociable. She's successfully maneuvered through a complicated, bureaucratic system with ease—a system that feels so clunky and foreign to Frankie even with her Reaper training completed.

Frankie suddenly feels as if she's sinking. It's a good thing she's dying soon because she wants the earth to swallow her up. She wants to disappear into the cool dark ground and live with the worms and her crushing feelings of rejection. Instead, she does something that comes easy: she acts like it doesn't bother her.

"Probably for the best," she says, inspecting her fingernails. "I'll be pretty busy for a while. Focusing on my career."

"Right," says Beau. "It's just..." He reaches out for her again, his palm against her cheek. He leans closer, his breath on her lips. "I—"

"Frankie!" her mother calls. "Now where has she gone to?" Her mother calls her name again, only her voice is closer this time.

Frankie is still looking at Beau when her mother rounds the corner, though, by tacit agreement, they have leaned back from each other. A respectable distance. A platonic distance.

"Frankie, darling. It's time," says her mother.

Frankie stands to follow her mother. Beau catches her hand before they turn the corner, before they rejoin the party and the eyes of her family.

He presses a kiss to her palm, and she instinctively curls her fingers around it, as if holding it tight, storing it for later.

"See you soon, Frankie."

And then she is gone.

OBITUARIES

Excerpt from the Hart Family's Annual Christmas Newsletter

We are so pleased to share that our daughter, Francesca, has officially been installed in her post as a Reaper.

Her certification ceremony took place on May 3, 1993, in conjunction with her eighteenth birthday. We are so proud of Frankie's accomplishments. She graduated in the top three percent of her Reaper certification course.

When Frankie isn't reaping, she enjoys reading, listening to pop music, and exploring Souls Town.

Excerpt from the Little Spark High School Chronicle, written by Penelope Church

Penelope Church, 17 and a half, was the victim of a brutal, unprovoked attack. The tragic demise of one of Little Spark High School's most popular students occurred on April 1, 1993.

She is mourned vociferously by her mother and her boyfriend, Little Spark High's own quarterback, Beauregard Astor.

Despite her young age, Penelope acquired a long list of achievements during her lifetime, including but not limited to:

- Volunteering at the local animal shelter
- Playing the lead in Little Spark High School's productions of *Romeo & Juliet, Music Man,* and *Rent.*
- Winning Miss Little Spark three years in a row
- Scoring 1583 on her SATs

Cont. on pages 14-16

Excerpt from the Applewood Bulletin

Eloise Brightly, 83, died on July 13th, 1994. She was born to Thomas John and Judy Marie Pendergast on November 13, 1915. Born and raised in New York City, Eloise Brightly moved to Applewood to live with her great-aunt after her parents were brutally murdered in 1925.

After arriving in Applewood, Eloise quickly became a vocal advocate for gopher tortoise conservation. She leaves behind one son, Stephen Brightly, and an ill-mannered tabby cat, Todd, that is currently up for adoption at the Applewood Animal Shelter for $100*.

*A representative from the Applewood Animal Shelter would like to clarify that the $100 is to be paid to the adopter. "There's nothing wrong with him. He's just spreading a lot of anti-authority propaganda among the rest of our feline guests. We think he'd do best in a single-pet home."

Excerpt from the Bramble Root Circle Newsletter

Matilda O'Brien, 30, passed away in the early hours of March 13, 1956, succumbing to injuries sustained from a gunshot. Matilda wasn't one for trivialities or frivolous sentiments, and, as such, this obituary will not indulge in such things. Matilda will be missed.

Coincidentally, her death does leave the Bramble Root Circle with a vacancy for coven bookkeeper. Interested parties may send their resumes to the address provided below.

Excerpt from Sun Ridge News, Channel Seven

A local man found deceased in his home was the victim of a brutal attack. Authorities say the man, identified only by the first name Alistair, was stabbed through the chest with a homemade blade bearing occult symbols. Police have requested anyone with information regarding this brutal murder to please call this dedicated helpline.

CHAPTER 7

A YEAR LATER

Eloise Brightly is walking down the sidewalk on a Wednesday afternoon in July, the concrete sticky with heat, when she quite suddenly stops.

There's no reason for her to stop. Not only has she not yet reached her destination, but she's only been walking for a short while, leaving her legs and lungs perfectly capable of continuing for quite a while longer before they call out for a pause.

She bends her head downward and, from a distance, seems to fall asleep, right there in the middle of the sidewalk on Heritage Lane, right next to the oak tree whose roots have slowly been encroaching on the sidewalk for a generation. Her shoulders lift and then fall back down in a heavy sigh. When asked later why she stopped then and there, she hadn't the foggiest.

Not that it matters in the grand scheme of things. It doesn't change the fact that, while standing on the sidewalk with her chin against her chest, and her shoulders drooping forward, a stolen vehicle originally owned by Hammersmith Security and Armored Car Services turns hastily around the corner of Main and Heritage, tires squealing.

As the truck careens to the left, the driver overcorrects, and powered by the momentum of its own weight and the anxious grip of the driver, the van continues to barrel on two wheels, up over the sidewalk and into the oak tree.

Eloise Brightly is knocked backward by a rogue tree branch. The doors of the van open, and as two figures clad in black jump out, so too do a million's worth of shiny copper pennies, fleeing their armored car like a hive of bees disturbed by an ignorant child. The avalanche smothers Eloise Brightly, the sound of a thousand copper voices in the wind muffling her startled cry. A second later, she is blinking at the face of a young girl with glasses so large that she resembles a frog.

Despite the fact that Frankie Hart knew exactly when and how she would die from the age of five, she still finds herself slightly surprised every time she wakes up in Death.

Death is cold and tedious, and if she had had any choice in the matter, she would have preferred to spend a little more time alive.

But, of course, family traditions must be upheld.

A year into her afterlife, she does not think on her death with any type of fondness. She recalls the surprisingly sweet taste of the drink her grandmother made for the occasion; the sugary liquid spread through her bloodstream like fire until she fell down, her lungs shaking with her final breath. The only good thing about the entire day was Beau and what has since been dubbed, in her own head, as the Moment.

The Moment was perfect, but it was fleeting. And so, she entered her afterlife with a broken heart and unshed tears in the corners of her eyes.

It's an honor to be selected for Reaper, as her Aunt Frank told her then, and, on some level, she agrees. Not everyone can pass Reaper training with such high scores. Not everyone can shed their earthly connections in order to transcend to a higher calling. Not everyone can walk to their death with their head held high.

And yet, she can't help but question why she had been selected for this role in the first place.

She's truly quite terrible at it.

She knew her first few clients would be difficult, as she navigated her newly appointed afterlife and job title. But, really, after a year of making this trip, she thought it would be easier by now. Sometimes, she almost wishes scythes weren't ceremonial.

Her standard uniform, sans scythe, consists of one wool vest (which she never wears), a badge (which she keeps in a smooth leather wallet in the inside pocket of her coat, next to her passport and a kind-of-sort-of-illegal Nokia flip phone purchased from a demon in a Souls Town back alley), and a standard-issue messenger bag linked to a pocket universe created for her own personal use.

The messenger bag holds all of her personal belongings, such as clothing, beret collection, a spare pair of glasses (just in case), a handful of hand-me-down coats, a tattered copy of the Reaper Handbook, and a surprisingly robust collection of grimoires and esoteric texts (also just in case).

In addition, there is a mini-fridge (which is woefully empty ninety percent of the time) and three tubes of lip balm floating around; there should be a fourth, but it appears to be lost.

She lives in a dormitory that she shares with

five other Reapers and despite the fact that she is hardly ever alone, either with a client or a roommate, she has never felt lonelier.

Frankie watches the Styx's impassive black facade ripple with incoming vessels as Eloise Brightly reminds her, not for the first time, that she is not fond of the cold. If you wore the coat I offered you, thinks Frankie, as Eloise runs her hands up and down her arms with an exaggerated shiver.

At first, Frankie was pleased to learn that her client was older. She had a young client last week who was tragic and rather unmanageable. It took her hours to convince the toddler to walk through the door, traveling from Life into Death where she would receive her housing arrangements and welcome packet.

An older client, however, would surely have already begun the process of accepting their death, being all that much closer to it. Right?

It didn't take long for Frankie to see the error in her assumption. Then again, if everyone handled their death well enough, Frankie would be without a job. One can dream.

Eloise Brightly, thus far, has proven even more unmanageable than the three-year-old, as she staunchly refuses to walk through the doorway, even after an hour of listing the benefits of doing so.

At long last, Eloise Brightly finally agreed to travel by boat, and so, here they are, in Souls Town, awaiting the *Stygian Jewel*.

The ticket booth attendant calls them forward and Frankie informs her that she is checking in with Mrs. Eloise Brightly of Number Four Breeze-way Court, deceased July 13th, 1994.

The attendant, a portly frog-daughter of Heqet named Carla, tells them to report to dock two to board the *Danse Macabre*. There is some confu-sion as Frankie attempts to ask what exactly is the *Danse Macabre* and why aren't they reporting to dock one for the *Stygian Jewel*.

The attendant croaks something about pennies and then calls for the next in line.

"It's your lucky day, Eloise," Frankie says. "We've been upgraded."

"I'm still dead. How is that lucky?" Eloise replies. "And it's Mrs. Brightly to you."

Frankie chokes back a retort and follows Mrs. Brightly through to the departure lounge, wondering when this whole Reaping business will get easier.

As she approaches the building, she experiences a familiar wave of dizziness. Although she faithfully fulfilled the required hours in Death needed to become a Reaper, her training did not dwell on the practical day-to-day procedures of the role. There was a highly prevalent assumption that she would need more experience opening a door directly to Death, and not so much experience taking the long way around, as she thinks of it.

In theory, the Reaping process should be simple. Someone dies, a Reaper shows up, provides them with the brochure and answers their questions. Then, they hold their hand while they walk through an officially sanctioned door, arriving right in the Next Step offices New Arrivals room.

With Frankie, the process seems to stall after the questions and before the door. She never seems to explain things quite the right way. She doesn't know how to comfort the recently deceased, and she's even worse at the hand-holding bit. Her familiarity with Souls Town is lacking, too, due to the fact that her training took place mainly in a cold, dusty office room at the Next Step offices. Even a year into the job, she still finds herself overwhelmed by the makeshift city that straddles the threshold between Life and Death.

As a result, Frankie can't help but think, not for the first time, that Souls Town is...weird.

Not weird in a spooky or intimidating way. It is like nothing she has ever seen in her life, and now, afterlife. The only way to describe the facade of the Souls Town gate is that it is, without a doubt, architecture. Not a particular style of architecture—just architecture.

Ionian columns, massive Neolithic stone blocks, red steel I-beams, and what looks like a palm tree trunk support a Buddhist stupa-cum-Mesoamerican pyramid topped with brightly colored onion domes and a glass Art Deco steeple. Bas reliefs from a thousand different human (and very much non-human) religions and cultures decorate the frontage.

There is Papa Gede raising a fat tumbler of coffee-dark rum to a bleary-eyed Shiva. A sprightly Mercury rubs the belly of doggy Xolotl while an uncharacteristically jolly Anubis attempts a few playful nips. Winged, stony-faced Azrael stands next to a stoical Izanami while both look upon the whole affair with detached bemusement. Surrounding the deities are a whirling mix of diverse daemons, sprites, satyrs, nymphs, fawns, and fae of every conceivable shape, size, species, gender, and arrangement of limbs and extremities.

And they are all moving.

To say that the storm of imagery is disorienting

would be to say that the Big Bang was a pretty decent light show.

There is, however, one image in the fantastical, metaphysical mess that remains still. The robed figure, larger than any other relief by several degrees, stands astride the entrance to the departure lounge.

This figure, Frankie knows, is Charon, the ferryman who carries souls across the River Styx to Death. Or at least, he used to. He hasn't been seen in centuries.

She wonders briefly what she would say to him if she ever met him. The stern, robed figure her family has followed for centuries, whose decree, filtered down through the generations, meant that one Hart must be sacrificed every third generation? She'd like to think she'd tell him what a jerk he is, but, truthfully, she probably wouldn't say anything at all.

Penelope Church is dead—but she's not going to let that get in the way of her social life. This is why, when the brochure for the new luxury cruise ship, *Danse Macabre*, fluttered its way into her path, quite literally, she didn't hesitate to fill out the section in the back and mail in her request for two first-class tickets.

The brochure, printed with the highest quality of purple dragon ink (much classier than hydra ink, which has the tendency to flake off if subjected to any measure of temperature fluctuation), proclaimed the many benefits of the ship over the standard ferries that call Souls Town their destination. However, it wasn't the gilded decorations, the centaur-leather chairs, or even the deluxe hot troll massages that drew her attention.

It was the proximity to Death's movers and shakers and the crème de la mort that Penelope craved. She convinced herself that her refusal to take the ferry with the hoi polloi was a practical choice—not a sign that she was a total snob. She needed a job, and the sort of folks that would take the *Danse Macabre* are also the sort of folks who could help her land one.

Souls-Town-on-the-Styx may not be the high society to which Penelope Church had been accustomed to while still alive, but it is difficult to start building a reputation of one's own while bereft of a family name in the cold realities of Death. She has the distinct feeling that, after a year, she will finally have the opportunity to get a foothold on the upper echelons of afterlife High Society after all.

She could have some business cards printed and finally begin her career as a personal stylist. So what if her clients may have hoofs or wings or fish tails or any amount of otherwise non-human style requirements?

She has a sketchbook filled with stylish solutions for the discerning dead; she just needs the connections to get started.

And frankly, the quality of the dragon ink bodes well.

She stands on the dock in Souls Town, looking down at the River Styx below, dark as blackberries. It reflects the stars like a mirror, and makes Penelope feel, briefly, that she is suspended in nothingness.

The sounds and smells of Souls-Town-on-the-Styx are never far away, and they quickly bring her back to reality. She is enveloped in controlled chaos, a rambunctious, yet steady mix of voices talking loudly, laughing, or yelling hoarsely, underscored by the gently lapping waves of the river that surrounds them. The air smells like seaweed and sulfur, with hints of fried batter and honey.

Her boyfriend, Beau, stands next to her. She's glad he agreed to accompany her. The tickets arrived while she was visiting him in Life, and she was already dreading returning to the coldness of Death for the umpteenth time. It's not that she misses being alive—being dead is really not that different from being alive—but the constant travel can be a burden on their relationship. She knows she should be grateful: not everyone is given a special issuance passport upon their untimely demise and not everyone has a boyfriend that would stay even after their death.

Their relationship has continued, more or less, as it had done so before. There have been some adjustments, naturally. The long distance, for one, means planning has to be meticulous, in order to maximize their time together until she has to travel back to Souls Town and renew her visa. And of course, it is rather bothersome that when she is in Life, he can't touch her, and no one, besides him, can see her. She relishes their time together, though. The warmth, the sunshine, the bright, vibrant colors.

Sometimes, she thinks about the moment when their paths converged upon the Passport Services office and how touched she had been to see him in the midst of the dreary grayness of Death, his whole countenance filled with warmth and something so beautiful it made her sad. It took her some time to realize that it was life that she saw in him. He is a warm presence against her side, and she is grateful for it.

Despite having a passport of his own, Beau has only visited her once. Penelope tries not to read too much into Beau's reluctance to visit her. He's been a bit aimless since he graduated high school, refusing to go to college and spending most of his time working at the coffee shop below his studio apartment.

Not that he needs the money.

The apartment is owned by his family, as is the coffee shop, and his parents are happy to have him living there if it means that he is working, instead of languishing away like his cousin Delia, whose idea of a busy day is spending hours by the pool drinking daiquiris and smoking cigarettes imported at great expense from Italy.

He's depressed, is all. And maybe still feeling guilty for her death, despite the fact that they established it wasn't actually his fault.

A bell rings in the distance, prompting a weather-beaten dock worker to call out, "Ferry!" He repeats the word in a couple of different languages, a few that Penelope recognizes but even more that sound otherworldly.

Perhaps this is because surrounding her on the dock are a variety of guests awaiting the arrival of a standard ferry, just as much as they may be waiting for the new luxury cruise liner, the *Danse Macabre*. A skinny fae with bright silvery wings stands next to a pointy-eared imp. An alligator wearing cowboy boots and a bolo tie converses with a cloven-footed nymph whose long golden curls hide her bare chest.

There are a few humans as well, including a man in a dark suit with neatly cut hair who had been very loud about how many coins he had won at a poker game the night before. "Enough to finally get me passage. It's only been twenty-bloody-years since I got here. 'Bout time."

Penelope wonders who will be boarding with her and Beau. Perhaps the confused vampire in the dark suit who looks quite rich, or the tall elven crea-ture with high cheekbones and eyes that look like silver ponds. They look quite important, she thinks.

Certainly not Frankie Hart, who is currently making her way through to the departure lounge with her elderly client in tow.

The dock worker yells "Ferry!" in one last lan-guage (Trollish, because naturally, you can't expect the eight-foot blue-skinned troll standing behind Penelope to understand English, let alone Spanish or French; as it is, however, Penelope knows that the troll, whose name is Oscar, is fluent in French and German, and is teaching himself Arabic).

The *Stygian Jewel* docks and a moment later, the cruise ship appears behind it. Much like the port-of-call that it serves, the *Danse Macabre* is helter-skelter with different cultural approaches to nautical technology.

While it is obviously large and luxurious, nei-ther Penelope nor Beau can quite work out how it actually moves. The boat sports a Polynesian outrigger, sails from a Chinese junk, the profile of an Age-of-Sail brigantine, and what looks like a figurehead from a Fae swan-boat. Penelope hopes Beau doesn't notice that bit; he abhors swans.

In the middle is a large blocky unit that houses three cabins on each side, with a dining area and observation deck up top.

Beau makes his way to the turnstile and converses with the ticket booth attendant. Penelope waits patiently and looks up at the shiny white mass of the cruise ship, pristine against the darkness of the river.

"You going to stand there all eternity, or do you want to get on the boat?" a voice croaks, bursting the bubble of Penelope's silent reverie.

Penelope wrenches her gaze away from the ship. Her eyes land on the ticket booth and its occupant. Not so long ago, the sight of a giant, surly frog in horn-rimmed glasses and gaudy naval garb straight out of a Gilbert and Sullivan operetta would have somewhat perturbed Penelope.

That was before she died, of course.

Penelope smiles at the amphibian ticket-taker. "Sorry, Carla. I was miles away for a—"

"We take drachmae, solidi, Kai Yuan Tong Bao, PayPal, Venmo—" begins Carla.

"—I know, Carla. I've got a passport, remember? We've done this several times now."

"We also take Visa, MasterCard, Diner's Club, pieces-of-eight, chicken bones, AmEx, gold florins, cowrie shells, dinars..." continues Carla without a lick of recognition for the person with whom she's had this exact same exchange several times.

"How about Discover?"

"Oh gods no. Who in their right mind takes Discover?" gurgles Carla, annoyed at the very thought.

"Well, I guess this will have to do," says Penelope, handing the clerk her passport to stamp.

Carla burbles and harrumphs, as she uses a disconcertingly raccoon-like paw to stamp the booklet.

"Next!" croaks Carla, causing Penelope to wince slightly.

Taking back her freshly stamped passport with as polite a "thank you" as she can manage, Penelope makes her way through the turnstile next to Carla's booth, and toward the door to the departure lounge to await the next leg of her journey.

"Right on time," she says, checking the faceless clock on the wall.

If pressed, Penelope will admit that Death is... not ideal. But she has made the most of it, even finding comfort in her routine. *Routines*, her mother told her once, *help us cope. A proper lady always has a routine.*

Of course, time doesn't mean anything in Death, so there isn't technically a natural way to divide the day. Instead, there is more of a vague, universally agreed upon window for starting one's "waking" hours. Penelope's "morning" starts with a good bit of stretching and calisthenics. Ectoplasm gets a little unseemly if it's not properly worked out. After that, despite lacking the need to actually eat, she has a healthy bowl of porridge with a splash of honey from the Trollish lands (trolls are renowned throughout the dimensions for their beekeeping skills).

After breakfast, it's time for Penelope's daily ablutions. Then, she has language study (Trollish; she practices with Oscar) followed by a light Caesar salad (she got the recipe from Nero, who's actually a lot nicer than you'd expect) for lunch, and on and on and on...

Routine, Penelope thinks, is what keeps Death livable.

CHAPTER 8

DANSE MACABRE

Matilda O'Brien has never once seen the merit of a routine. At least, not after she found herself *Quite Dead*. Life was another story entirely, one with rules and carefully measured morsels of times dedicated to rather specific things. For instance:

6:45 am to 6:47 am: brush teeth.

3:46 pm to 4:02 pm: peruse the latest *Reader's Digest*.

5:16 pm to 5:45 pm: Eat dinner—chicken, Brussels sprouts, and one glass of milk.

One can imagine her surprise, when, on a clear summer's day, Matilda O'Brien was shot straight through the chest with a hunting rifle illegally acquired by the neighbor's son. After all, it had not been on the day's schedule.

Perhaps if she hadn't been quite so focused on following her routine, she wouldn't have been standing right there, in front of the window, when Billy sneezed at the last second. His rifle, originally aimed on a rabbit by the tree, found a new target at the most inopportune moment.

Death had been an unexpected release from the routines of Life (this point was, in fact, the first on the list of pros and cons she requested from her Reaper when she died), and as soon as she stepped foot in Souls Town, she swore to never stand by a routine again.

Of course, this proves quite difficult, where, in her duties as Second Assistant Courier, she finds herself beholden to ferry schedules and appointment times.

This is why Matilda O'Brien is late.
Again.

Of course, it doesn't help that clocks are non-existent in Death, appearing as a solid white circle, despite the maker's intention. She rushes through the departure lounge, squeezing by the short girl with huge glasses and her elderly companion. She's not as lucky as she passes by a couple, one tall with glossy black curls, the other just as tall, though only because of her shoes, with long blonde hair. As Matilda collides with the boy—the dark haired one—she drops the package she is carrying for a client and hears a gut-wrenching rattle from inside the wooden confines. The brown wrapping paper rips as it lands.

The boy picks up the package, looking at the exposed corner with a furrowed brow. She nods a thank you as she accepts the package, wondering if the dark-haired young man gleaned too much from that tiny corner. It would be fitting, she thinks, to have her career ended because of a small tear of paper.

She doesn't have time to properly worry

though. She skids to a stop at the front of the *Danse Macabre*.

"Ticket," she says to herself, patting her pockets. "Ticket, ticket… Ah, ticket!"

Ticket stamped, she makes her way onto the vessel, balancing her suitcase and the rectangular package, her hand clutching at the corner as she tries fastidiously to keep the tiny flap of torn paper from revealing too much of the box's contents.

The horn of the *Stygian Jewel* sounds in the distance, reminding Matilda why she is boarding a cruise ship in the first place. She had been quite distraught when she realized that the ferry had been fully booked and about to leave. It is imperative that she deliver this package on time.

Carla had almost gurgled with amusement at Matilda's predicament. "There's a room left on the *Danse Macabre*," she suggested with a hiss.

Matilda contemplated the schedule board. Technically, the trip on the cruiseship will take more time; the boat's course will take them along the Gorgon's Trail, which circumnavigates a tiny, unnamed island between here and there, and which the standard ferries embarking from Souls Town typically travel through the middle of, making liberal use of a series of lochs built centuries ago. The view around the island, of course, is rather more picturesque, so she supposes it makes sense, in the grand scheme of things.

Yet even accounting for the detour, the *Danse Macabre* is scheduled to arrive in Death proper only a day later than the *Stygian Jewel*. If she were to wait for the next economy ticket out of Souls Town, she would be waiting two days, arriving in Death proper *three whole days late*.

One day seems like a much smaller sacrifice.

Yes, she can make do with just one day late.

She paid for the ticket with her own money, trying not to balk at the price. Though she must admit she is getting her money's worth. On the *Danse Macabre*, even the diamonds are gilded. The floors are sparkling, freshly polished wood. The scent of lemon cleaner hangs lightly in the air, and she lets her fingers trail against the smooth gold railing as she makes her way down the walkway to the cabins.

When she finds her room (Cabin Three, starboard), she locks the door behind her and places the package on the bed. She sits next to it and places a hand atop the box.

"Everything will be okay," she says to the empty room. "We'll get there on time."

The sound of violins, tinny and hectic, crinkles its way out of the speaker affixed to the wall in the corner. Beau sips his drink, the smooth finish of whiskey coating the back of his throat.

Although the whiskey is of the highest quality, he wishes it was a cigarette. Despite the fact that he told Penelope he would quit, he still packed a box, and he reaches into the pocket of his coat—the old army coat that belonged to Frankie's grandfather, the one he wore when they first ventured into Death and which he has since begun to claim some sort of ownership over—and fingers the corner of the cardboard packet, wondering vaguely if anyone on board has a lighter.

Penelope, of course, doesn't need a coat. She sits next to him, pale and beautiful in a sleeveless dress that tucks in at her waist and then flows down her legs in a satiny pink fabric. Frankie, on the opposite side of him, doesn't technically need a coat either, but she wears one anyway, tugging it around herself like armor. To be honest, Beau would be quite sad if Frankie wasn't wearing her coat. She wouldn't look like *Frankie* without it, her round glasses, and her crooked beret.

The dining room of the *Danse Macabre* reminds Beau of his grandmother's house. The walls are a dark navy, dotted with golden decorative anchors. The settee in the corner is upholstered in an emerald velvet that looks pretty but uncomfortable, and the wood floors are covered in plush rugs with aquatic motifs. The round rug, in the very center of the room, features a large squid whose tentacles reach out to the edges. On the opposite side of the room is a smaller table covered in green felt for playing cards. Against the back wall is a well-stocked bar, rows of variously shaped bottles glistening in the soft light of the room.

The dining table is placed parallel to the windows that stretch across the far end of the room, showing the dusky river beyond. The glossy wood of the table is inlaid with a winding marble design that Beau assumes replicates the current of the river, or possibly even a snake.

"Thank you all for attending the maiden voyage of the *Danse Macabre*, sponsored by William Shakespeare in honor of his latest play *Othello in Space*." The captain of the ship, an alligator named Jasper, motions toward the stained-glass section of the window that depicts an image from the play. The two figures embroiled in a glowing-sword fight glance away from each other to lightly bow in the direction of their audience before returning to the intense gaze of battle.

"Please, enjoy dinner," says Jasper, with a sweep of his arm. His drink (a cocktail called Pond Water that is probably delicious but suffers from a very unfortunate color) splashes onto the table. Jasper doesn't notice as he smiles and holds his glass up in cheers. The guests raise their glasses in turn.

Beau can't eat or drink anything produced in Death, which is why he packed his own provisions, his duffel bag filled more with protein bars and large flasks of water than clothing. He unwraps his protein bar as the food appears on the table for the more pulse-challenged guests.

The liquor, however, has all been imported from Life and seems to have the same effect on the dead as it does on the living. Pushing the craving for a cigarette to the back of his mind, Beau tries to savor another sip of his drink, tasting notes of smoke, caramel, and cinnamon on the tip of his tongue.

Frankie is sitting on his right, and he recalls, briefly, the last time they were in Death together. After spending more than three hours stuck in a waiting room at the Passport Services office, Beau had very dearly wanted to kiss her.

He has since done that, of course.

And he would very much like to do it again, if he's honest with himself.

He wonders not for the first time why he's here at all, let alone with Penelope. He recalls the conversation he had with Frankie at her Death Day party. She told him she was going to be too busy for him. He should have challenged her. He should have pointed out that he could see the fear in her eyes but that it was going to be okay, because whatever death brought, he would be there with her, to help her through it all. He should have broken up with Penelope before he went to the party. He should have...He should have done so many things. Then again, he knows Frankie well enough to know that she would not have taken kindly to such honesty. She might have even said the same thing; he's fairly certain she has a fear of commitment and intimacy.

Her dismissal of the kiss, no matter how false, still makes his chest hurt. She took the easy way out, but so did he. He went back to Penelope, told he loved her, and swore to himself to never tell her about the kiss with Frankie. He took the coward's way out, and he comforted himself with the thought that Frankie did the same.

It still doesn't change his feelings for her. But, honestly, he's not sure how to end his relationship with one dead girlfriend, if only to start a relationship with an equally dead girlfriend (assuming, of course, that Frankie wants to be in a relationship with him).

His etiquette classes didn't account for this particular situation.

Really though, as far as dead girlfriends go, the arrangement with Penelope is surprisingly doable.

Despite the fact that Frankie has a passport and certain privileges that come from her position as Reaper, her main priority will forever be her job and it's true that it keeps her busy. Though they speak often on the phone (a brick-like chunk of plastic that Frankie bought him for his birthday; a sticker on the back claims it can reach at least four other dimensions, but they have not had a chance to test that yet), in the year that she's been working as a Reaper, he has only been able to see her twice. At least with Penelope, she can visit Life and stay a while.

Besides, if he's being completely honest with himself, he still feels the burn of guilt at the back of his throat when he thinks about Penelope's death. He knows it was Frankie's spell that killed Penelope, as far as the paperwork goes. He can't help but wonder if he did have a part in it, though. Perhaps his mango-tini brought her to Death's door, allowing Frankie's spell to give her that last push over the threshold. Penelope had been incredibly allergic to mangoes, after all.

Regardless of who is at fault, Penelope's death did something he never thought possible: it brought Frankie back into his life.

Frankie Hart—who was his best friend when he was a kid.

Frankie Hart—who was his first kiss.

Frankie Hart—who he is probably, most likely, in love with.

The whiskey has gone to his head, he thinks, and he sits his glass down, his hand returning to his pocket and to his pack of cigarettes.

He glances at Penelope who is sitting on his left. He leans against her slightly, feeling the weight of her shoulder pressed against his. She gives him a distracted smile and a pat on his knee. It had been quite the shock when she first visited him in Life, only to find that she is not-quite-solid. If anything, he might get lucky on this trip, he thinks, but the thought does little to bolster his mood and even less to assuage his guilt over his current predicament.

As the other guests tuck into their dinner, Beau chews his protein bar and looks around thoughtfully. There are only three other guests on board, including Frankie's client, Mrs. Brightly.

The elderly woman sits beside Frankie, her face wrinkle-lined and shrewd, crystal-blue eyes scanning the table with scrutiny. When Mrs. Brightly's inspection ends at Beau, he smiles politely and nods his greeting. She scowls at him.

She scowls deeper at Frankie, though.

The recently deceased vampire across from Beau looks wary but still mildly amused by the proceedings as he sips a spoonful of soup. His eyes light up briefly, before flickering shut in lightly concealed appreciation. The cut of the vampire's suit and the sharpness of his jawline remind Beau of his own father, a stilted sort of elegance that speaks of clipped tones and well-practiced sneers.

The skittish middle-aged woman beside the vampire is the same woman who nearly knocked into him and Penelope earlier. She nervously brushes back a small tendril of hair that's escaped her braid and takes a delicate bite of her dinner. All of her movements seem fragile and fleeting, like a butterfly hopping from one petal to the next. He's fairly certain she's carrying some sort of contraband based on the symbol he saw on the package she dropped; surely, anything with a skull stamped on it is illegal?

There doesn't seem to be any other staff besides the captain. The food appears on the table, and their drinks are automatically refilled as Beau discovers just now, when he sits his glass down, only to lift it up again and find it filled to the brim. The room is silent, awkwardly so, and the sound of silverware clinking against porcelain begins to annoy Beau.

"So," he says, breaking the silence, "Why don't we introduce ourselves? My name is Beau Astor and a fun fact about me is that—"

Penelope clears her throat and gives him a curt shake of her head. "This is not the place for ice breakers," she says, *sotto voce*.

"I was just trying to get to know the other guests," he replies between gritted teeth.

Frankie clears her throat. "My name is Frankie," she says, addressing the room. Her cheeks are slightly pink, or at least, he assumes they are. To him, they look gray, like a storm cloud, and he smiles gently as she picks up the conversation he started. "I'm a Reaper. My client was upgraded, which is why we're here. A fun fact about me is that I am a descendant of the Charon Order. Which is why I'm here. Why I'm a Reaper. In the first place."

"Way to name drop," mutters Penelope, unkindly.

Mrs. Brightly puts down her fork with a clatter, and pretends to arrange a stray blue-rinsed curl behind her ear. "Well, I guess I'm next..." Her tone is reluctant, but her words flow easily.

Perhaps too easily.

While Mrs. Brightly talks about her childhood in a New York City brownstone ("I don't remember much, but we lived on Woodruff, right across from the church, on the third floor and our phone number was—"), Beau glances down at Frankie. "Thanks," he says, bumping his shoulder against hers.

Her cheeks turn darker, a lovely shade of dove gray. "Of course." She takes a small sip of her drink, the corners of her mouth threatening to turn upward. He understands the feeling, as he attempts to school his expression into something neutral, something other than what it wants to do, which is smile with giddiness.

The conversations flit around them and while Beau catches wisps of the words and the stories held within, he feels, for a moment, as if it is just him and Frankie. They are far away from the *Danse Macabre* with its cold marble tables and gilded fixtures that look tarnished to his eyes.

He is swept away by her, lost among the waves of the Styx and he is quite happy to be in such a state for an eternity.

"How are you?" He favors her with a smile,

pleased when she returns it so easily.

"Oh, you know." She shrugs lightly, glancing away for a moment. He knows the movement so well; it means she is going to tell him the truth even if she's embarrassed by it. "A little too dead for my liking but okay otherwise. It was nice of you to begin the introductions. I can't imagine spending two whole days on this ship with complete strangers."

"A proper Astor controls the conversation," he says, affecting a voice that sounds eerily like his father. "Plus, I hate awkward silences."

The introductions move onward to the vampire. Beau briefly registers that the vampire's name is Alistair and that he was brutally killed by a vampire hunter, or so he believes ("I think I remember a knife or perhaps a stake. There were symbols on it, I remember that much.")

Beau leans closer to Frankie. "How's your latest client handling Death?" he asks, his voice barely above a whisper.

"She keeps complaining about the cold," replies

Frankie, leaning closer so she can keep her voice low. "I gave her a coat, but she refuses to wear it."

Beau smirks and takes a sip of his drink. "She seems like a handful."

Although he saw her in the departure lounge, Beau takes a moment to look at Frankie up close. She looks tired, he thinks. Can dead girls be tired? They're probably more tired than alive ones, he supposes.

"I lived there for some time, too," says Mrs. Brightly suddenly. She seems startled that she's shared this tidbit, though Beau thinks it's a false sense of modesty; she was perfectly able to share information about herself during her introduction. "But I don't remember you," she adds.

"The memories of mortals can be a fickle thing," says Alistair, in what Beau feels is an unnecessarily enigmatic tone.

"Before I died, I had never been outside of England," says the middle-aged woman. She introduces herself as Matilda. "I had plans to travel when

I was younger but something always got in the way. I would have loved to visit New York, especially. It was the forties then, and I've heard the loveliest stories from others who were there. Of course, now that I travel all the time in my job as Second Assistant Courier, all I want to do sometimes is stay home."

"Where is there to travel in Death?" asks Mrs. Brightly, keenly.

"Oh, mostly my travel consists of this—a ferry between Death proper and Souls Town. However, there are a few other realms that branch off of Souls Town, and of course there are the other rivers, which have places all their own. I've been lucky enough to see things like the Great Opal Falls of Faerie and the Storm-Keep of Perkunnos."

"That sounds quite lovely. Are those places as cold as here?" asks Mrs. Brightly.

"The cold fades," interjects Penelope, knowingly, waving her fork in the air for emphasis. "It takes a bit of time, but you'll get used to it."

Beau takes another sip of his drink, only to find it empty. He sits his glass back down on the table with a heavy thud.

"What about the flashbacks to...well, my death?" asks Alistair, sheepishly.

Penelope nods. "Those fade too, though I still occasionally wake up in the middle of the night feeling like I'm suffocating." She casts a glance in Frankie's direction. "But really being dead isn't all that different from being alive." Penelope pauses and adds quietly, almost to herself, "Though maybe that means I was doing something wrong. There should be some difference between the two."

"Oh, I don't believe that hogwash," says Captain Jasper with a hiss. "Death and Life are two sides of the same penny."

Mrs. Brightly winces ever-so-slightly at the mention of pennies.

"Which side is Life and which is Death? Heads or tails?" asks Matilda, with an amused smile and a hiccup of a laugh. Her drink, too, is empty. Her cheeks are a deep charcoal gray.

This begins a rousing debate.

"Well, now I think—" says Mrs. Brightly.

"Oh, I imagine it would be—" begins Penelope.

"I vote for heads for Death, personally—" interjects the captain.

Beau glances at Frankie who is listening to the debate with a detached sort of interest. He's seen that look on her face before, usually in Chemistry class. He watches as she adjusts her glasses, pressing a knuckle against the corner of the frame to push them further up her nose.

He is startled away from his observations when Penelope's hand on his thigh brings his attention back to the table. "Sure," he says, in answer to a question half-heard.

Penelope scowls. "You didn't hear the question."

"Sorry. It's the whiskey. Bit distracted."

She makes an unconvinced noise in the back of her throat. "Maybe if you weren't drooling over

Frankie, you'd pay more attention to your girl-friend," she says, her voice low and scathing.

"Maybe the whiskey is getting to you too, Penelope." He shoves his chair back, the screeching unheard amongst the ongoing debate.

"No, I still think Death is the heads of it all," Matilda is saying, with a shake of her head.

"I'm inclined to agree with Captain Jasper on this one," says Alistair.

"Where are you going?" hisses Penelope.

"To find a lighter," he mumbles.

CHAPTER 9

A Storm Rolls In

The waters of the river are tranquil, broken only by the hull of the *Danse Macabre* as it moves forward. The slight shift in the cool waters brings a wave of warmth over the creature below the surface.

The kraken, who often thinks of herself as Luella (her name in the native Kraken language, Akkarish, is practically unpronounceable without a siphon, beak, and a couple tentacles), awakens slowly, stretching languidly, casually making her way to the surface. When her head pokes up out of the water, she blinks against the brightness of the constellations above as she takes note of her surroundings. River quadrant 3, she thinks. Along the Gorgon's Trail.

The ship is just passing by her now, and she can tell it is on its first voyage. It still smells new, and she can feel it against her tentacles, a light touch of iron and paint. There's no rust or barnacles; the hull of the *Danse Macabre* shines almost as bright as the stars.

She blinks, mentally calculating the number of souls occupying the vessel. Six...No, seven. One of them is still alive, and she almost didn't recognize its song, which is an awkward, jittery sort of tapping rhythm.

To be alive in Death was once an unusual thing, but it has, in her experience, become marginally commonplace since the establishment of the Passport Services office, bringing a handful of living souls to these waters over the past few centuries. Regardless of permissibility, she has always wondered what would bring a live soul to the cold waves of the river. Why not use the passport to pass through a sanctioned doorway?

Oh yes—she knows about the doors. Her tentacles are everywhere in these waters, and she remembers a time when doorways were forbidden and Souls Town was nothing more than a broken piece of wood and a reluctant traveler.

Curious, she creeps forward, her tentacles brushing against the bottom of the hull, tasting the metallic tang of iron and something else—a sweet pomegranate tinge that reminds her of the Cocytus. She had a sister who lived there once; perhaps she should visit soon.

She presses forward, moving in pace with the ship and—yes, there he is, she thinks, looking through the window of Cabin Two. Oh, he's young, she realizes quickly. Though, strangely, his soul is roughly three hours older than his body.

That's the price to pay for traveling in cold waters like these, she thinks. She watches him through the window as he stares blankly at a young woman. Despite the fact that the young woman is dead, Luella can tell that she is stunningly beautiful. She looks like sunshine—something Luella hasn't seen in a very long time indeed.

There's something strange about her light, though. It seems to expand outward, much like Luella's tentacles, particles of energy sparking against the very fabric of Death.

How odd.

As Luella watches, the young man says something that makes the woman's shoulders hunch upward in a defensive stance. Then, he shakes his head. The woman takes a step forward, but then stops.

Whatever he says next, makes her take a step away from him, as if being cornered by a predator. He reaches for her, but she backs away, her hair whipping around her shoulders as she shakes her head.

He gives her a steely look and then stuffs his hands into the pocket of his coat, before leaving the room. Luella watches for a second longer, sees the young woman collapse on the bed in tears, and then redirects her attention to the young man, who is walking along the open pathway between the cabins and the railing that marks the edge of the boat.

A few feet behind him, she sees another figure, shorter, but wearing a coat just as bulky as his, walking quickly. The second figure is too busy glancing behind them and a moment later, the inevitable happens: the second figure bumps into the young man with a gruff "Oof."

A word or two is exchanged, though Luella can't hear the specifics. The second figure pushes past the young man and a moment later, they disappear around a metal staircase.

Luella keeps her focus on the young man this time. He sighs, then follows in the same direction as the second figure, yet turns sharply to make his way to the port side of the *Danse Macabre*.

Luella dips back below the surface and pushes herself underneath the ship, to pop her head up on the other side, just in time to see the man knock on Cabin Five.

When the door opens, she can just make out the silhouette of another young woman with short dark hair. Not as attractive as the other one—the shining one the man was with before—but powerful. A witch, she thinks. One of Charon's chosen, though her bloodline is so far diluted, she probably doesn't realize the power humming inside of her.

The witch lets the man into her cabin and closes the door. Unfortunately for Luella—but fortunately for them, most likely—the curtains are closed.

He doesn't stay long, however. Luella, still infinitely curious, follows his shadow as he makes his way up a wrought-iron circular staircase and into a room on top. A light flicks on, filtering through the stained-glass mural that adorns the balcony doors, casting rainbow-colored shadows against the water below. The doors open and the young man walks out, carrying a bottle of caramel-colored liquid and one glass. He pops open the bottle and pours a healthy splash into the glass. He leans against the railing and looks out at the inky-black expanse before him.

Can he see her, she wonders? Most likely not, she decides. Her camouflage is quite good and living boys don't often have the best eyesight. As she has heard, they often fail to see what is right in front of them. Then again, she's heard the same about dead boys, so maybe the state of living isn't really the issue.

Suddenly, Luella sees a second shadow sneaking its way closer to the young man, looming behind him as if to swallow him up. She thinks about raising a tentacle to let the young man know he has company, but before she can move, the newcomer makes a strange sort of lunging motion toward the man. There is a shout, the sounds of struggle, a grunt of effort, and then a plop.

Something has fallen into the water, and she dips back below to reach a tentacle out, to rescue the object from the deep and return it to the man.

But when she pokes above the surface again, the man is gone, as is his attacker.

The next day dawns dark, as do all days on the river. There is just a haze of purple where the water meets the sky, a suggestion of dawn, a nudge of a new day.

Penelope awakes alone, a flush of regret tingling down her body as she remembers her words from the night before, thrown harshly and without care, and yet with the exact precision of a professional archer; she knew they hit their target when he gave her a steely look and left.

She stubbornly went about her nightly routine, removing her makeup as she mumbled justifications for her words. She continued to hold onto her own sense of righteousness as she slipped angrily under the covers and tugged them up to her chin. After a moment of thought, she shifted to the middle of the bed and spitefully tucked the quilt around her, so that when Beau returned, he would be forced to sleep on the very edge and without a blanket.

She let her consciousness wander into sleep, waking only once to readjust the blanket. She did not wake up enough to realize that Beau still hadn't returned to their cabin.

So, when her alarm goes off in the morning and the edges of the bed are cold and empty, whatever comfort she took from being right fades quickly.

Penelope slips out of bed to go in search of Beau. She starts with the dining room, which she remembers having a small seating area tucked into the corner. She assumes he went in search of a lighter, found a bottle of whiskey, and passed out on the small settee.

Yes, that's most likely, she thinks, because where else would he go to sleep?

The realization that there is another place he would go hits her so forcefully, she almost misses a step as she makes her way to the upper deck. She grips the metal railing and continues up, as she wishes, with a false sense of hope, that Beau is snoring away obnoxiously in the dining room, and not in someone else's bed.

And yet, when she opens the door, the room is empty. She does, however, find a crumpled pack of cigarettes on the bar, next to a conspicuously blank space where a bottle of whiskey should be.

"Italian," she mumbles to herself, noting the expensive label on the cigarettes and the sweet clove smell in the air. He was here, at least.

Out on the observation deck, she finds a broken glass, its former contents spilled over the edge of the boat in the night. She picks up a wedge of glass and sniffs. Notes of smoke and caramel and an earthiness that makes her grimace.

She lets the glass fall back to the deck as she grits her teeth, fingers clenching in anger or anxiety, or, most probably, something more akin to heartbreak.

She makes her way through the dining room and back down the spiral stairs to Cabin Five, on the port side of the boat. It was foolish of her to even check upstairs. She should have gone straight to Frankie.

Because that's clearly what Beau did.

That's what Beau will always do, she realizes, as she knocks on the door with little care for the slumbering occupants inside. She doesn't care that she might wake the other passengers either. She knocks louder, thinking about the weird twisted thing Beau and Frankie seem to share; they are tangled up in each other, and Penelope can't ignore it any further. She refuses to be treated this way—

The door swings back, right as Penelope is about to knock a third time, and Frankie stands in the doorway, blinking sleepily while hiding a yawn.

Frankie adjusts her glasses with her free hand and blinks again. "What—?"

"Where is he?" Penelope shoulders her way into the room, noting the mussed sheets, the articles of clothing strewn on the floor, surreptitiously searching for something of Beau's. The door to the bathroom is open, the lights turned off, but, still, she peers into the dark tiled room, takes note of the single, lone toothbrush resting against the edge of the porcelain sink.

Frankie is frowning as Penelope turns to face her. "I don't know what you're talking about," she says sleepily, shrugging on her coat over her pajamas.

"Beau. He wasn't in our room and he's not in the dining area."

"Maybe he's watching the star-rise on the deck?"

"He's not there."

"Are you sure?"

"I'm not blind."

Frankie arranges her beret on top of her messy bob and hides another yawn. "Well, maybe you just missed him—"

"He didn't come back to our cabin last night. Are you really telling me that he didn't come here?"

Frankie's cheeks turn pink. "I didn't—it

wasn't—that's not what—that's not what happened. He was here, but then he left."

"When?"

"I don't know. I didn't think I'd need an alibi."

"Frankie, if you're—"

"If I'm what?" asks Frankie, rummaging through her messenger bag, "Lying? Penelope, why would I lie about this?"

"I don't know. You tell me." Penelope watches as Frankie leans further into her bag, up to her shoulder. "What are you doing?"

"Looking for my phone—ah, here it is." She pulls the phone out and tosses her bag onto the bed. Penelope waits while Frankie navigates to her contacts and hits the send button. She leans in close to listen, and Frankie angles the phone so they can both hear. It rings for a few agonizingly slow seconds and then an error noise sounds followed by a friendly female voice saying, "We're sorry. This number is out of the available service range and could not be reached."

Penelope makes a small grunt of frustration. "Well, he must be here somewhere. He wasn't in our cabin. He wasn't in the dining room or on the upper observation deck."

"What about the lower one?" offers Frankie.

Penelope narrows her gaze and crosses her arms. Then, she turns swiftly on her heel and leaves.

Frankie follows after her, tugging her coat tighter around her body. They skirt the metal staircase that leads up to the dining room and make their way through a large porthole that acts as a door to the lower observation deck.

They are confronted with the inky dark dawn of Death, broken only by the lone figure of Captain Jasper in his neatly pressed white jacket and navy striped shirt. He takes a puff of his pipe and exhales the smoke slowly as he watches the constellations twinkle into existence, awakening from their slumber.

"Captain Jasper! Have you seen Beau?" asks Penelope.

Captain Jasper jumps slightly at the forcefulness of Penelope's tone, but recovers quickly, shaking his head with a hiss. "Not seen anyone today besides you two."

"Where could he be?" she mumbles, looking out at the horizon. She isn't sure if she's asking the two beside her or some abstract concept of fate. As Frankie and Captain Jasper talk, she repeats the phrase quietly to herself, like an incantation. She grips the railing, feeling the breeze whip her hair around her shoulders. She licks her lips, now coated with a thin layer of salt from the river, and she asks it again, as she watches the purple in the distance continue to bloom in the sky, like ink dropped in water—and yet the few constellations that have awoken are rapidly being covered by dark wisps of clouds and the wind seems to shift, picking up force, turning colder.

"Where else could he be?" she asks, and this time, she aims the question at Frankie.

Captain Jasper answers. "There's an empty

cabin. Have you checked there?"

The empty cabin is at the end of the row on the port side of the boat, Cabin Six. It shares a wall with Mrs. Brightly in Cabin Five and a back wall with Alistair, who is on the starboard side in Cabin One. Penelope wrenches the door open without knocking, but the room is dark and empty.

"Maybe he's..." begins Frankie, biting her lip in thought. She lets her arms fall down to her sides with a shake of her head "I don't know," she admits. "Is there anywhere else on this boat to hide?"

Captain Jasper considers this but ultimately shakes his head. "Unless he's in someone else's cabin."

"So, we wake everyone up," says Frankie, glancing worriedly at Penelope. Outside, a low rolling boom of thunder spreads out around the boat, shaking the windows. The wind screams against swan figurehead. "We'll meet in the dining room and do a head count."

The atmosphere in the dining room is tense; the guests of the *Danse Macabre* were not expecting to be so rudely roused by a teenage girl demanding their presence so early in the morning, and after a particularly late, drink-heavy night, too.

"Where is he?" she demands, standing in the center of the room with hands on hips and lips trembling with unshed tears.

The dining table is already laden with breakfast, and the passengers are silent, sharing pointed looks with furrowed brows or wide-eyed confusion.

"Beau seems to have disappeared," clarifies Frankie. "Has anyone seen him this morning?"

"Up until a few minutes ago," says Mrs. Brightly, reaching for a piece of toast, "I was sleeping in my cabin. We all were. When would any of us have seen him?"

"Maybe he got locked in a broom closet," suggests Matilda, taking a bite of her scone. Behind her, the stained-glass windows darken to navy blue and burnt umber as purple clouds edged in green gather in the sky, stealing away what little light there is. The orange-tinted light bulbs in the dining room cast a warm haze in contrast. Outside, the wind picks up, and the ship wobbles over the waves with a creak of protest.

"Maybe he fell overboard," says Alistair, before taking a sip of his tea.

"More likely he was pushed," mumbles Mrs. Brightly.

A crack of lightning reverberates against the advertisement for *Othello in Space*. The two swordsmen look nervously toward the horizon.

Penelope crosses her arms. "What does that mean?"

"The walls are thin, that's all," replies Mrs. Brightly. She turns to address the room. "They were arguing well into the night. I think we should ask her what they were arguing about."

"That's none of your business."

"And anyway," begins Frankie, clutching the corner of the bar as a wave knocks the boat about. "Beau is an excellent swimmer. There's a lifeboat on the other side of the ship. He could have swum around and climbed back up."

"What if he was unconscious?" asks Matilda. "He could have drowned. Or been eaten by the kraken."

"I think Luella is vegetarian these days," interjects Captain Jasper.

"If he died, he'd still be here," points out Penelope. She looks at Frankie. "Right?"

Frankie nods. "Yes. But he might not be *here* here. He could be back at Souls Town."

"So, we just wait," the captain says, with a clap of his hands. "The boy will probably make the journey over on the *Stygian Jewel* and you'll see him again in no time."

A roll of thunder echoes around the room, swallowing whatever Penelope had been about to say. Captain Jasper looks out the windows and hisses.

"That storm is coming in quick. We won't be able to see the stars soon."

"Is that bad?" asks Frankie, pushing her glasses further up her nose.

"Let's just say that I've been navigating these waters longer than you were alive, and I've never encountered a storm." His green complexion looks pale, bordering on sea foam.

"Not one?"

"Never. It doesn't rain here, this far out from Souls Town."

"Then why is it raining now?"

"It doesn't matter," says Penelope, suddenly, as she plops down on the settee. Her voice is dull as she adds, "He's gone."

"Penelope, I'm sure he'll be—"

"No." She shakes her head. "He's gone."

Her declaration is joined by the patter of raindrops against the darkened windows of the *Danse Macabre.*

Penelope watches the rain slide down the window in her cabin. The *Danse Macabre* is anchored; the weather conditions have turned the river unnavigable and the captain has decided to wait out the storm.

Could Beau have fallen overboard, Penelope wonders. He's an excellent swimmer but if he was drunk and hurt himself...who knows? Not to mention whatever lies beneath the depths of the river—something could have snatched him up before he made it to the lifeboat. She has seen tentacles rise from the river's inky depths and, once, while on the *Stygian Jewel*, she saw a whale tail break the surface.

But even if he succumbed to some creature of the deep or he drowned, Penelope knows what happens when one dies. "He should still be here," she says to the nearly-empty bottle of wine sitting next to her.

She takes a sip, hardly tasting the dry apricot and plum flavors.

He must be in Souls Town, like Frankie suggested. Or maybe he's on the ferry making his way to orientation? Maybe he's in Death proper already, waiting at her doorstep. She should have given him a key to her place months ago.

She can't stop thinking about his words from last night, can't stop the defeated, dull tone of his voice from echoing in her mind as he shook his head and asked, "Do you want me to die for you?"

The memory of her reply, so final, her voice too high-pitched with emotion, stings as it comes back to her. "Yes."

A crack of lightning brings her back to the present, and she looks apprehensively at the window, watching as the raindrops chase each other down the glass. The captain had been equally concerned about the storm and somewhat baffled too. She recalls a similar look on Mr. Fergus's face in the Next Step office as a crack of lightning struck the branch outside. She thought little of it at the time; for all she knew of Death, it could be plagued by rogue lightning bolts.

She can do the math, however, and adding together the worried expressions with the lightning then, and now this storm, she can see the common variable.

Her.

She feels a flush of fear, which corresponds with a boom of thunder that shakes the window. There's something wrong with her, and she crumples into tears again, overwhelmed with the knowledge that she is a terrible girlfriend and a dysfunctional ghost and she can't do anything right—

A knock on her cabin door startles her. "Who is it?"

"It's me. Frankie. We need to talk."

She doesn't reply.

"Penelope, please." Frankie tests the door handle and finds it unlocked. She makes her way into the room cautiously, closing the door behind her with a quiet click.

Penelope sniffs and refills her glass. "You were the last one to see him, weren't you?"

"I think so, yes—but Penelope, it's not what it sounds like. He came to my room, but only to talk. He didn't stay long."

"And why should I believe you?"

"Because he wouldn't do that to you."

Frankie's words settle between them and for a second, Penelope isn't sure what to feel. She is numb with too many emotions. Then, she begins to cry in earnest, burying her face in her hands.

A moment later, she feels Frankie sit down next to her, the bed shifting slightly with her weight. Another moment of hesitation, and then Frankie's hand is on her shoulder, so light it might as well not be there.

"He mentioned you fought," she says quietly.

Penelope's voice is muffled as she replies. "It was stupid. I was just being jealous and petty. I wouldn't kill him just because we argued."

"I know. You're far too strategic for that."

It takes Penelope a few seconds to place Frankie's tone, a mix between sarcasm and honesty. Penelope looks up, startled, but finds Frankie's smirk to be more amused than cruel. But then Frankie's mouth turns down into a frown. "But something happened to him last night, and I don't think it was an accident."

"What do you mean?"

Frankie leans closer and whispers, "I think Matilda is hiding something." She glances to the door, as if worried about who may be on the opposite side. She shifts closer. "Last night, he told me that he saw Matilda in the hallway and that she looked skittish, like she was hiding something. Doing something she wasn't supposed to be doing. He also said that he thinks she's carrying something illegal."

"The brown package she dropped before she boarded?"

Frankie nods.

"So, you're saying Beau saw something that he shouldn't have seen, and Matilda killed him to keep him quiet?"

Frankie shrugs. "People have killed for less."

"True. So, what do we do?"

"We investigate."

"Together?"

Frankie grimaces and adjusts her glasses. "Look, I know we don't get along. I know...I know I'm the reason you're here and I apologize for that. I'm truly sorry. But we both care about him. Something happened and we're the only ones who care enough to ask questions. Besides, we're stuck here for the foreseeable future—might as well make good use of our time."

Penelope briefly wonders if she should share her theory about the storm, but something stops her. What if she's wrong? One problem at a time, she thinks. Instead, she says, "Shouldn't we call...I don't know. The police or something?"

"Death doesn't really have police." Frankie

scrunches her face in apology. She uses a knuckle to adjust her glasses again. "At least, not for things like murder, if that's what happened to Beau. Not much point considering most everyone here is dead already. Which makes it all the more important that we investigate. The River Guard won't care." She shifts, bending her leg up onto the bed so she can lean closer to Penelope. "If he was murdered, we're the only ones who will care. I won't stand by and let someone get away with that."

Penelope purses her lips in thought. Frankie's right, of course: if Beau died, it's really just a matter of finding him. The broken glass by the edge of the upper deck points toward Beau falling overboard, but she has never known him to be a clumsy person, even when drinking.

She ponders Frankie's theory about Matilda. If Frankie is right, and Matilda did have something to gain from Beau's death, then it's plausible that she took matters into her own hands. She can't imagine the slim, nervous woman overpowering Beau enough to toss him overboard, but perhaps she has some special power? Perhaps, in much the same way as Penelope controlling the weather, Matilda has super strength? Maybe superpowers come with death and it's so commonplace, no one talks about it. Then again, maybe Beau didn't fall overboard. Their fight last night comes back to her, haunting her.

Do you want me to die for you?

Yes.

Could Beau have done something stupid at her behest? The thought sends a shiver down her spine.

Regardless, Penelope does want answers.

But can she work with her own accidental-murderer to solve this mystery? Maybe, she thinks. Frankie knows more about Death than she does. It's her job for Charon's sake.

And what would Penelope bring to the table? She isn't a detective. She's a personal stylist. She takes a moment to eye Frankie's attire, to note how her shoulders slump forward to fill up the bulk of the coat, broken up only by the messenger bag slung across her chest.

It's not a terrible coat, perhaps if she rolled up the sleeves and paired it with a slimmer-cut pant? Frankie's face is almost completely hidden by her glasses, which is a shame, since her eyes are a lovely shade of green. The beret she wears is lopsided, but even Penelope can admit that the angle is surprisingly chic.

Frankie grimaces under Penelope's scrutiny and tugs the coat tighter around herself. "What?"

"Oh nothing. I just wonder if maybe you should be wearing a deerstalker instead of a beret." Penelope places her wine glass on the bedside table and sits up straighter, decision firmly made. "Right, well, first thing we need to do is find what Matilda is hiding, and see if it's worth killing over."

Frankie nods. "Right. I'll search her cabin if you can keep her occupied."

"Why can't I search her cabin?"

"Because you're better at talking to people."

Penelope raises an eyebrow at the compliment, whether it was intended as such or not. "You're right," she says. "I'm far less socially awkward than you."

For a moment, Penelope worries that her words are a little too harsh (one of the things Beau said last night is that she can be cruel at times, a hard truth that she is trying to acknowledge and atone for) but Frankie just smirks. "Truer words."

CHAPTER 10

INTERMINABLE DAMNATION

Matilda leans away from Captain Jasper but doesn't quite escape without a few drops of wine on her sleeve. Captain Jasper continues undaunted.

"We have been forsaken by Charon," he is saying. He's been talking about their current predicament in various metaphors, using increasingly more hyperbolic phrases each time. "We are lost in the Kraken's Lair," he says, with a shake of his head.

Matilda takes a sip of her brandy. "I don't think it's all that bad. It's just a bit of rain."

Captain Jasper continues, as if she hadn't spoken. "It is an ill day when the fires of Hades reach up into the sky and the clouds succumb to the depths of the Styx."

Matilda ponders this one for a moment, not entirely certain of its meaning. She glances about the dining room as Captain Jasper continues, unbidden by his lack of attentive audience.

She and the captain are sitting on the settee, her embroidery long forgotten on the small table in front of them.

On the opposite end of the room, Mrs. Brightly is playing cards with Alistair at the green-felt table. The soft sound of the cards being shuffled around is a nice accompaniment to the patter of rain against the windows.

Matilda actually finds it quite soothing. The force of the storm has slackened but the gray veil of rain still shrouds the boat. They might as well be suspended in nothingness.

The boat rocks gently in the waves. She hopes it continues to be so gentle; she gets terrible motion sickness.

Matilda continues to nod along to the captain's voice, hardly listening to the words, until she spots Penelope entering the room.

She waves her over, using the opportunity to shift further down the settee and out of the "splash zone."

Penelope settles in between them, clutching a tissue and sniffing delicately.

"Penelope, dear. I'm so glad to see you. How are you holding up?"

Penelope's cheeks flush with worry. "I couldn't stay in the room," she says, lips trembling slightly. "Not with his things...and..." She sniffs again and dabs at the corner of her eyes.

"Of course," says Matilda, putting an arm around her shoulders. "We're all sorry for your loss. I'm sure he'll be found soon. Perhaps he is waiting in at the Next Step offices?" Matilda gives Penelope another squeeze. "It's been known to happen."

"Has it, really?"

"Well, not that I've ever heard but I'm sure...

how about a small glass of brandy? To take the edge off?"

Penelope nods gratefully and dabs at her eyes again. "Thank you everyone for being so understanding. I know this isn't how any of you expected this trip to go."

"You know what they say, we plan and the ghouls in Administration laugh," says Matilda, as she makes her way to the bar. She scans the bottles lined against the wall, a finger to her lip as she mumbles the names to herself. "We appear to be out of brandy. I have a bottle in the bar in my room. Be back in just a moment."

"On second thought," says Penelope hurriedly, "perhaps I shouldn't drink alcohol just now. Maybe some tea?" She dabs at the corner of her eye again.

Young women are odd, Matilda thinks. Even dead ones—especially dead ones.

Matilda asks if anyone else wants tea, since she is making a pot anyway, and Mrs. Brightly happily accepts, her attention wavering from the card game.

Alistair doesn't seem too put out. A quick glance at the arrangement of cards, and Matilda can see why. He was losing.

Tea is prepared promptly and each of them accepts their gilt-rimmed white teacup. Matilda settles back down on the settee, next to Penelope. Captain Jasper adds a healthy amount of whatever is in his flask. He offers up the addition to anyone else, but only Mrs. Brightly accepts the offer.

The face she makes after a sip tells Matilda that she made the right decision.

"So, with all of this fuss," begins Penelope, "we haven't finished introductions. What is it you do with your afterlife, Matilda?"

"We've already been over this, dear," says Mrs. Brightly. "She's a delivery person."

"Courier," corrects Matilda. "Second Assistant."

"Oh, that sounds fascinating." Penelope blows delicately on her tea to cool it down. "What kinds of things do you courier?" She raises the cup to her lips, pinky out.

At least she has decent manners, thinks Matilda, bringing her cup to her mouth in the same manner. "A little bit of everything." Matilda glances away, toward Captain Jasper.

"You know, I think we may have been on the *Stygian Jewel* together, once," continues Penelope. "You look familiar. I do a little bit of frequent travel myself."

"Indeed? I do typically take the normal ferry, but I got my times a bit mixed up." She laughs nervously. "There was a room available here, so I took it. I was supposed to—"

Matilda's answer is forgotten as Captain Jasper makes a grunt of alarm and loses his balance, spilling his tea right into Penelope's lap. Penelope jumps up with a hiss; the tea is still quite warm.

"Oh, I'm so sorry. The waves—rough water!" Captain Jasper chuckles nervously, reaching for a napkin. "Here, let me—"

"No, it's okay." Penelope closes her eyes briefly,

and then, with jaw clenched, she says, "I think I'll just go clean up." Penelope leaves in a rush, still carrying her teacup.

"What a strange girl," mumbles Matilda, settling back against the settee, as she takes another sip of her tea.

"Where do you think the other one has gone off to?" asks Captain Jasper.

"I don't know. We haven't seen her in a while."

"Fine by me," says Mrs. Brightly. "She's a bit of a bore, that Reaper girl."

The rain continues to beat down on the windows. Alistair returns his attention to the deck of cards and begins to shuffle. Mrs. Brightly nods reluctantly at his silent invitation. Matilda sips her tea and watches the normally still waters of the Styx pebbled with raindrops.

Captain Jasper once again takes up his laments, his voice underscored by a large clap of thunder in the distance, "Oh, what strange waters are these! We have seen better days!"

Penelope walks quickly to her room, the tea stain now cold against her thighs. She slips inside, dropping her heels by the bed and rifling through her suitcase. She bundles a new skirt under her arm, slips on a pair of ballet flats, and then glances out the window to make sure the hallway is still empty.

She leaves her room, closing her door as quietly as possible, and makes her way to the opposite side of the boat. She doesn't bother to knock before entering Cabin Five, though she does let herself in with one last look behind her to make sure no one has followed.

Frankie is sitting on the bed, leaning against the headboard with arms crossed grumpily. She shakes her head at Penelope's expectant look. "She must have hidden the package somewhere else on board." She motions toward Penelope's stained skirt. "What happened to you?"

"Captain Jasper happened," she says, flicking

her hair over her shoulder. She makes her way to the bathroom to change, leaving the door slightly ajar as she tells Frankie what happened. "I was making real progress with Matilda, until the captain spilled his tea in my lap. He claimed it was because the boat rocked, but—" She leans out of the bathroom, hand braced against the frame, "—there wasn't a swell. No one else felt it."

"Maybe he's just drunk? He's always taking sips from that hip flask," suggests Frankie.

"Maybe," admits Penelope. She steps out of the bathroom, arranging her new skirt. She flicks off the light and then sits primly on the edge of the bed, handing Frankie the stained skirt. "Does that smell like alcohol to you, though? I don't think our captain is nearly as drunk as he pretends to be."

"Why would he pretend though? What does he gain from that?"

Penelope shrugs. "It means we underestimate him, at the very least. He flies under the radar. And the only kind of people who want to fly under the radar are the ones who don't want to be seen."

Frankie bites her lip as she considers Penelope's new information. "Beau said Matilda was heading down the hallway, away from her room."

"The hallway that ends with a metal staircase that leads up to the captain's quarters."

"Or the dining room and through to the upper deck. Or, she could have stayed down, and made her way through to the lower deck."

"Did Beau mention if she was holding anything? Maybe she threw whatever it was overboard?"

"Maybe," says Frankie. "But not likely. If it was something worth killing for, I should think she would keep it close by."

Penelope nods. "And there was nothing in her room?"

"No sign of the box she was carrying when she boarded."

Penelope frowns and shifts, so that she is sitting next to Frankie, legs outstretched. "So, what do we do now?"

"Wait until after dinner," Frankie adjusts her glasses and looks at Penelope. "When everyone else goes to bed, we can search the lower and upper decks."

Penelope matches her gaze. "And if we don't find anything?"

"We'll look somewhere else. We'll keep looking until we find something."

Dinner is a solemn affair, a far cry from the lively conversation of the night before. The rain continues, the boat sloshing drunkenly about on the waves as a feral wind whips its way around the bow.

The thunder is a constant in the background, rendered mundane by sheer frequency. Captain Jasper has put aside his hyperbolic assertions for the time being, acknowledging the fact they are truly and properly stuck.

"I bet this isn't how you expected this trip to

go," remarks Alistair, sipping his wine. "You said this was the maiden voyage of the *Danse Macabre*, yes?"

"Indeed," says Captain Jasper, in between sips of split-pea soup. "Though I have sailed these waters for many years on many vessels."

"Is it true that the marble in tables were imported from the Shaydo Islands?" asks Matilda, a spoonful of soup half-raised. She doesn't seem to notice that the spoon is tilted, the soup spilling down with a plop. "I've been to the Shaydo Islands and it has the loveliest views." She brings the spoon to her mouth and frowns.

"Yes, yes," says the captain, with an excited hiss. He begins to describe the process of transportation and drilling and the permits they had to acquire. "And the ghouls in Administration said that we didn't need the specialty fabric for the window dressings, but, then it was impressed upon them—"

Frankie sighs, more out of habit than necessity, and looks out of the window, but she isn't seeing the storm outside or the river turned pale gray with rain. She's seeing the absence of Beau; he should be sitting next to her, obstructing her view.

He should be sitting next to Penelope, she corrects herself. She feels the knowledge like a lead weight in her chest.

When she suggested they work together to discover what happened to Beau, it was out of necessity. Frankie may be good at sneaking around and fading into the background, but Penelope is good at observing people, at getting them to open up. Frankie knew she wasn't going to find the answers alone.

She wasn't prepared for the way it amplified her feelings of guilt and regret, though. The Moment flits through her thoughts, an almost constant presence at the back of her mind, but the memory turns sour as she notices Penelope's tear-stained cheeks.

Frankie never thought she'd be the type of person who would kiss another girl's boyfriend, but that's exactly what she did.

Add in the fact that Frankie is responsible for said girl's death and well...if Hell was a place, she probably deserved to be there.

She looks over at Penelope, who is discussing the merits of cool tones versus warm tones and how the dark, rich blue of the wall compliments the warm-toned light bulbs in the fixture above them. Frankie can't help but think that Beau made the right choice.

He needs someone like *her*. Someone graceful and cunning. Someone with a keen eye for detail and the expertise to back up her opinions.

Penelope is the complete opposite of Frankie, who is a tiny introvert with too big feelings and glasses that make her look like a frog, whose mouth is too loose with her opinions with zero expertise to back up her bravado, who has never once been accused of being graceful or cunning in any way, shape, or form.

Frankie, who played with mischief and ended up responsible for Penelope's death. Frankie, who misses Beau so much it feels like a pang in her side. Frankie, who will never know Beau as anything more than a friend.

She will be okay with that, she tells herself, as long as Beau is there. Just have to find him, first, she thinks.

The scraping of chairs against the floor brings Frankie's attention back to the room and to the fact that dinner has ended. Frankie looks down at her plate, realizing she's barely touched her food and yet finds that she doesn't have an appetite anyway. She pushes away from the table and stands, biting back a yawn as the weight of her feelings suddenly crashes down on her in the form of fatigue.

A second later, Penelope is gripping her arm so tightly, Frankie feels much more awake.

But while the force of Penelope's grip gives her a jolt of alarm, it's the frantic words whispered into her ear that truly wake her up: "Matilda shouldn't know so much about this boat."

What a funny business—this Death, Alistair thinks with a silent scoff. Then again, Alistair never considered himself worthy of Death in the first place.

He had been a vampire for so long, he'd forgotten the certainty of the thing. He spent all two hundred years of his interminable damnation with this forgotten entity, giving very little care for how his actions might be perceived by those around him and even less care for how they would affect those around him.

He lived with blood permanently crusted under his fingernails, the mineral tang stuck to his clothes. And why shouldn't he have spent his time on earth like that? His damnation was a gift, presented to him by a siren in the night, a slip of a spirit who was foolish enough to entrust upon him this cherished, precious thing called immortality.

He took advantage of it as frequently as possible, until, one day, even the sheen of blood began to fade. He grew weary of the violence, even wearier of the constant shifting, moving from place to place to avoid persecution for his crimes.

He bites back a yawn, as he has been doing since he arrived here. The movement is still wonderfully quaint. Sleep has eluded him for centuries. He is looking forward to resting his eyes, to drifting off among the stars, even if they are just in his mind. Maybe tonight he will have a dream.

He settles into bed, grimacing at the wrinkles his suit has acquired since he arrived. Although he amassed a large amount of wealth during his interminable damnation (thus the reason he could afford his ticket aboard this fine aquatic vessel), he didn't have time to do any shopping while in Souls Town.

He hopes to find an acceptable tailor when he arrives at their destination.

He distracts himself from the state of his attire, by recalling the last dream he had. It was the night he was Turned and it had been entirely mundane (so mundane, he can't recall any specifics), but he had been awoken by a sound in the night, his heart beating frantically against his chest as he came face to face with a demon.

Not really a demon, of course, as he learned later—but a vampire.

And thus, his fate was sealed.

He descended into the night with his mistress, wearing the evidence of his crimes as a medal. He was proud to be a vampire, one of the select few creatures blessed with eternal life. When he shifted away from that lifestyle sometime in the mid-1980s, he retired to Florida, living in a Gulf-side bungalow surrounded by bougainvillea and palm trees.

Although the reality of his true nature had been difficult to hide at times, his attempt was admirable. He tried daily to be a productive member of society. At the time of his death, he had been a volunteer for the public library and had just auditioned for a part in a play being put on by a local theater group.

He was good friends with his neighbor, Evelyn,

who often invited him over for tea. They had an ongoing puzzle spread out on the kitchen table, and they would chat, casually linking pieces together over a bottle of wine.

He worries briefly about Evelyn. Who will cat sit for her when she visits her son in Cambodia? Or help her water her hibiscus? Will she finish the puzzle without him, or sweep the pieces, loose, back into the box?

He's not sure which he would prefer.

Alistair slowly drifts off to sleep with thoughts of puzzles and cats and his neighbor's hibiscus in full bloom, the sound of the seagulls calling out in the late evening sun.

He can just about hear the sound, feel the breeze on his cheeks, and taste the tea, piping hot.

He can feel the warmth of the tea against his sternum—but then the warmth fades, and pain spreads through his chest as the unmistakable sound of a knife being sunk into muscle and bone echoes in his ears.

Penelope may be graceful, Frankie learns, but she is far from nimble. "You're being too loud," she whispers.

There is a soft huff of a reply before Penelope takes another step, this time gentle and slow, and yet her ballet slippers still scuffle against the floor. "Better?" Penelope whispers.

No, thinks Frankie. "Yep," she says. "Let's start upstairs."

The metal stairs creak under their weight, so Frankie slows her movements, evenly placing one foot on the step before raising the other one. Penelope follows behind, with more grace but far less care. Once in the dining room, they split up, heading toward opposite ends of the room to begin searching for Matilda's brown package.

Frankie lifts a pillow on the settee. "Tell me again what Matilda said." Finding nothing hiding behind the pillow, she crouches down to look under the settee and even stretches her arm forward, to sweep the ground.

"She asked a very specific question about the furnishings of this ship," hisses Penelope, rummaging through a storage chest in the corner. "But earlier, she implied that she was here purely by accident."

"I see," says Frankie, ducking behind the bar.

"Exactly. I think it's imperative we find this box." Penelope comes to stand near the bar, leaning over it to see Frankie. "It could be proof that she has something to hide."

Frankie straightens and places her hands on her hips. She nods. "Let's check outside on the deck."

Penelope leads, easing open the glass door but holding it open for Frankie to pass through first. The air is cold outside, the rain making the floor slick. Staying just under the overhanging to avoid the rain, Frankie glances around, looking for potential hiding spots and is rewarded by the rigid shape of a storage box butted up against the wall, in a small nook, out of the way but not out of sight.

She rummages inside, sifting through life jackets and rope and a few other articles of nautical accouterments. She closes the lid and pushes it to the side, wondering if there is anything shoved behind it.

The box is heavier than she realizes, and she grunts as she tries to push it. It moves an inch. She stands, wiping at a strand of hair stuck to her forehead. "Hey, Penelope, can you help me—"

"There's something out there."

Frankie turns, following Penelope's gaze as she peers out into the rain. There is a dark green glow in the distance, and for a second, she thinks she sees a strange movement in the water, a shift of something that goes against the wind, a small parting of waves.

Frankie blinks and begins to take a step forward, but then suddenly, there is a shout. The light downstairs flickers on.

Penelope grips the sleeve of Frankie's coat "What was that?"

"I think it came from Alistair's room."

Penelope looks at the knife sticking out of Alistair's chest and frowns.

"My suit is ruined," says Alistair, motioning toward the knife, which wobbles slightly. He is still in bed, propped against the headboard, legs crossed indignantly. He attempts to fold his arms across his chest, to further display his disgruntlement, but the knife is in the way, and he drops his arms to his side with a huff. "I will require compensation from whomever is responsible for this."

The attack on Alistair is concerning, and Penelope shares a look with Frankie: what are the odds that this second incident is unrelated to what happened to Beau?

Penelope doesn't believe in coincidences. Or

at the very least, she thinks true coincidences are quite rare. She gives Frankie a curt nod.

Frankie leans down and looks closer at the knife sticking out of Alistair's chest. "The same bone handle as the ones in the dining room." She adjusts her glasses and looks up at Alistair, motioning toward his chest. "Mind if I...?"

Alistair nods his agreement, and Frankie grabs the knife with both hands, pulling it out in one smooth movement. Alistair immediately glances down, fingers probing the spot. His skin is smooth and unmarked, but the suit remains damaged.

Penelope leans over Frankie's shoulder and narrows her gaze at the tear in the fabric. The suit is Italian-cut, quietly expensive, in a simple charcoal wool. "I could fix that up for you. Just a few well-placed stitches and the jacket will be right as rain."

"An ironic turn of phrase," mumbles the captain, glancing out of the window. The rain is still pelting against the boat, droplets pinging off of the metal like bullets.

Matilda scoffs, even as she reaches for some-thing to steady herself. "There are more important things than your suit, Alistair. Like the fact that someone here is trying to kill us off."

"Now, I highly doubt that," says Captain Jasper. "Perhaps it was a mistake?"

"Well, it's nothing to do with me," says Mrs. Brightly. "I was in my room, sleeping, which is more than I can say for those two." She motions toward Frankie and Penelope.

"What is that supposed to mean?" asks Penelope, arms crossed. Lightning flashes outside, and the boat sways. She reluctantly unfolds her arms to grasp at the bedside table, steadying her-self. She keeps her gaze narrowed at Mrs. Brightly.

"It means," begins Mrs. Brightly, a hand against the wall as the boat rocks forward again, "that Alistair shouted and we all came running out of our rooms, but these two came from the staircase."

"We were having a drink in the dining room, if you must know," Penelope replies easily. "And anyway, you got here pretty quick, considering you were asleep."

Matilda clutches the edge of the armoire, hand on her stomach. "I think I need to lie down. All this rocking..."

"This isn't helping," says Frankie, looking a little green herself. "Why don't we all just pause for a moment?"

"Indeed," says Captain Jasper, gripping the doorframe. "I think we should all make our way to the dining room for a drink. To relax."

"And to determine everyone's alibis," adds Frankie, shooting the captain a pointed look.

"Of course," he concedes, motioning for every-one to leave the room.

They make their way to the dining room, walk-ing along the rain-slicked pathway as waves crash into the hull, covering them all in a fine mist of brackish water. The lights are off in the dining room, and Frankie hopes no one remembers Penelope's earlier lie about them being in here.

Thankfully, it seems everyone's mind is on Alistair's attack, and no one questions why one of them would have had the wherewithal to turn off the lights while rushing to investigate a shout of alarm. Not to mention the fact that there is no evidence of them having a drink, no half-empty glasses of wine or chairs pulled out from the table.

Beyond the deck, the green sky and the dark black river stretch out into an abstract arrangement of angry shapes and muted colors. The boat sways with the water. A crack of lightning briefly illuminates the room, casting eerie shadows against the wall.

"We are securely anchored, yes?" asks Alistair, hand against the wall as he makes his way to the card table.

Captain Jasper nods. "Yes, I don't think we're going anywhere."

"The storm does seem to be getting worse," points out Matilda, clutching her torso with one arm while gripping the edge of the bar.

Mrs. Brightly, seated by the window, waves away Matilda's concerns. "This is nothing. Why, I remember a storm, when I was—"

"Is there any way to get in touch with the River Guard?" asks Penelope, looking sternly at the captain.

"—the waves were higher than we were," continues Mrs. Brightly.

Alistair nods politely. "That's fascinating," he says to Mrs. Brightly, yet his attention is on Frankie whose introspective expression shifts into something more pointed. "You have an idea?" he asks her.

"It's not really an idea," she admits, with a shaky smile. "A theory, I suppose. I can't open a door stable enough for one of us to pass through, especially with the storm getting worse, but I may be able to open a door long enough for us to throw a message through."

"Through to where?" asks Penelope.

Frankie shrugs. "Most anywhere, I suppose.

The River Guard, maybe? But again, I don't know if it will be stable enough."

"What would our message say?" asks Mrs. Brightly.

"That someone's been murdered and another has been attacked. We should request law enforcement," replies Penelope.

"Is there anything that can be done about the storm?" asks Alistair.

The captain hisses. "Weather events like this don't happen. I'm not sure the River Guard would know what to do."

Frankie adjusts her glasses. "Could the River Guard even make it through the storm to get to us?"

The captain shrugs. "They might be able to file a request with Administration?"

She's not entirely sure that Administration has the power to disperse a weather event (she's not even really sure who the Administration is, if she's being honest).

Is there a form for that? She wouldn't be

surprised. There are forms for everything in Death.

"I think it's worth trying, dearie," says Matilda. "I would very much like to be back on a solid branch."

The boat creaks as if in agreement.

CHAPTER 11

HERE AND BACK AGAIN

They spend some moments crafting a message. Penelope transcribes their request on the back of a *Danse Macabre* brochure because she has the best handwriting.

To Whom It May Concern

The Danse Macabre has been waylaid by a most unfortunate weather event. Additionally, one passenger has gone missing (presumed dead—he was alive when he boarded—it's complicated—will explain in person) and another has been attacked with a knife. We humbly request your assistance with this matter.

Sincerely,

The Passengers of the Danse Macabre, *Souls-Town-on-the-Styx's own luxury travel vessel. To book, please send a carrier-bat to the following address:*

Souls-Town-on-the-Styx
Revitalization Committee Headquarters
Mortuary Row, Suite 567,
Souls-Town-on-the-Styx

When the note is complete, Penelope folds it neatly in half and hands it to Frankie, who is looking anxiously out at the river. "What do you need us to do?"

"Stand back," says Frankie, with a small smile. "Opening the door is easy enough, but I don't know what will happen after it appears. As far as I know, no one's ever attempted to call up a door in open waters."

"What are some possible scenarios?" asks Penelope quietly. She can see the worry in Frankie's face and although she doesn't know much about Reaping, she does know a thing or two about stage fright. It wouldn't do for Frankie to forget her lines now, so to speak.

"We could all get sucked in and transported somewhere. Maybe it's Souls Town, or maybe another realm entirely. Or I could accidentally create a black hole and destroy all of Death."

"Valid concerns. But what's most likely?"

"The first?"

Penelope raises an eyebrow. "Or...you succeed. That's what's most likely." Penelope grasps Frankie's shoulders. "Look, I know our history is tumultuous at best." She ignores the scoff. "But I do trust you, Frankie Hart. You will open this door. It will be stable enough to toss that message through." She leans in closer, so that only Frankie can hear her next words. "You will get us to safety and we will find Beau."

"How are you so sure?"

"Because you love him as much as I do." Frankie's surprise is clear on her face. "I'm not blind or stupid. Beau has many faults, but his loyalty is not one of them. He cares so much for you, Frankie."

"I'm sorry. I hope you know I would never try—I would never want to come between you two."

"I know. We'll deal with all of that later. After we find Beau." And then, before Penelope can change her mind, she pulls Frankie into a rough, quick hug. "You can do this."

Frankie nods, looking steadier than before. Penelope joins the other passengers as they arrange themselves in a semicircle at the back of the dining room.

From where Penelope is standing, she can just see a sliver of Frankie's cheek, her eyes shut tight in effort. The boat tilts again, and Penelope is forced to take a step back reaching blindly for the top of the settee.

Frankie steps forward. She stands in the middle

of the room with her back to the group. She faces the glass doors that lead out onto the deck, and even though the two swordsmen have long since retired, the terms of their advertising contract now expired, Frankie is still framed in dappled patterns of the blues, greens, and reds they left behind.

Frankie's coat bunches up at the shoulders as she raises her arms, palms facing forward, and she leans ever so slightly, as if pressing against a wall. The boat tilts again, and Penelope's focus shifts past Frankie for just a second. She squints, taking in the view beyond the dining room doors. The ever-roiling shadows shift back and forth like snakes, white-capped and heavy.

Frankie's hands glow like coals, white-orange palms, fingertips soft pink. Penelope wrenches her gaze from the window and watches as Frankie brings her hands together, palms pressed and arms stiff. The air seems to vibrate. Slowly, as Frankie brings her hands down in a precise slicing motion, a door appears in the middle of the dining room.

Although, Penelope can't help but think that the word "door" is a somewhat loose definition of the twisted, gnarled tree trunk that's appeared. Really, the only thing that makes it a door is the shiny gold knob in the center, surrounded by pale, mottled bark. Upon closer inspection, however, she sees that the mottling is actually bone, woven into the grain, as if the tree had grown up, around, and through a cemetery.

As Frankie takes a step forward to grasp the handle, Penelope's focus shifts again, just for a second, on the river beyond. Belatedly, she realizes that the shadow she saw earlier had not swept along with the same regularity as the waves—but had actually moved counter to the river.

And now, as Penelope blinks, her mind attempting to catch up with her eyes, the shape rises up like a snake poised to strike.

"A tentacle," she whispers, eyes darting between the new arrival and Frankie, whose attention is fully on the door in front of her. Penelope has barely a second to react—and too late, the tentacle lands against the side of the *Danse Macabre* with a loud thunk. The weight of it tilts the boat closer to the water, the boat creaking with the effort.

Everyone and everything on board begins to slide, feet losing purchase as hands grapple for something solid. The ship makes another ominous sound of protest. The tentacle reaches up again, dripping inky black water onto the deck. It wraps around the railing, using the boat as leverage to pull itself closer. Another tentacle reaches up and thwacks against the glass door, which swings open obligingly.

The weight of the creature pulls the boat even more toward the water, and Frankie's door begins to slide away—with Frankie still holding onto the handle. Penelope tries to reach out to grab the back of Frankie's coat, but her fingers only brush against the waxed canvas before Frankie and the door slide out of the dining room, onto the deck, and over the railing.

The resulting splash is lost among the sound of lightning striking the Styx.

The water should be cold, but it isn't. Frankie once read that people don't feel wetness; they feel temperature. If it's the same for the dead, then the river must be the same temperature as her, because she feels nothing.

She is suspended, hair tangling with seaweed, her beret dislodging from her head. She feels her glasses begin to slide away as well, and she clutches them, holding them firmly to her face as she sees the blurry door sink down into the unknown depths of the river. She doesn't know where the message has gone, but there are more important things—like not joining the door on its journey to the bottom of the Styx, if a bottom even exists.

Fear grips her chest with the reminder that she can't swim, but she takes some comfort in the knowledge that she can't drown. She pushes her free arm down as she kicks, still clutching at her glasses, in a direction that she feels is most likely to be "up."

When she breaks the surface, she swipes frantically at her glasses, wiping away the droplets of dark water, and wondering, perhaps, if she hit her head—because she is no longer floating in the Styx, or at least not in the same part of the river that she fell into. The *Danse Macabre* is nowhere to be seen. The surface of the water is smooth, the skies above clear and fathomless.

In front of her, the water ends, gentle waves lapping at a smooth surface that slopes upward. She kicks toward it, feeling her feet connect with stone. Up close, she can tell that it isn't as smooth as it appears. It is delicately hatched for optimum grip, and she pulls herself easily to her feet, taking measured steps out of the river. She finds her beret dancing on a wave and stuffs it into her pocket for safekeeping.

After being on the *Danse Macabre* for two days, she feels a little wobbly on solid ground, so she pauses to look at her surroundings while her body acclimates to the lack of motion. Further still, after hours of incessant stormy soundtrack, she finds that she misses the noise, the gentle rolling thunder, the pitter-patter of rain drops. The atmosphere here—wherever here is—is oppressive, almost a physical presence against her temples. The molecules have sat still, undisturbed by another's presence, for too long. They have grown weary and heavy with boredom.

Another step brings her to the top of the slope and into a rather messy...bedroom? Or at the very least, there is a bed: a four-poster frame standing proudly in the middle of an oddly shaped room with awkward corners and random curves. The floor is the same as the ramp she stands upon, a dark polished onyx, though the hatching fades as she moves away from the water.

The room is largely filled with books, stacks

swaying precariously as they reach toward a ceiling sparkling with unknown constellations. There are other objects too: whirling mechanical contraptions, piles of keys, cutlery, stacks of cabinet drawers overflowing with random assortments of objects, tape players with tangled cords, shiny coins and wrinkled dollar bills, shoes missing their partners, and even, at the base of a pile close to her, a rusty bicycle with rainbow tassels affixed to the handles.

There is a window, too, on the wall directly opposite from her, though whatever is beyond is so dark, she can see nothing but her own indistinct reflection.

So confused and slightly enamored, her curiosity prickling at the sight of such eccentricities, it takes her some seconds to realize that she's not alone. She blinks at the man standing beside her. His dark, messy hair makes her think of Beau, but his skin is paler, ivory white, and his eyes are the same black as the river. He looks roughly the same age, but stands at least an inch taller than Beau. He's dressed in all black, a frock coat over a black waistcoat and black shirt, tucked into slim black pants. A very realistic snake is embroidered in shimmering silver thread along the high-necked collar of the coat, circling around twice to drape along his broad shoulders.

"Who are you?" he asks.

"Who are you?" she replies. Her words echo around them, dancing mockingly like a third presence in the room.

He takes a step closer to her, dark eyes narrowed. "I asked you first."

"Tell me where I am and maybe I'll tell you my name."

"You're Here," he says impatiently. "How did you even get Here? You shouldn't have—who are you?"

"I'm Frank—" she begins to say, but her reply is cut off as a thick, green tentacle wraps around her midsection and pulls her away.

She reaches out, more out of instinct than any real attempt to save herself from being dragged back into the river, and clutches at something—anything. Her fingers wrap around cold metal. She has only a brief moment to realize that she's grabbing at the necklace slung around his neck, before the kraken's strength becomes no match for the silver chain. It snaps in two.

He lunges, eyes wide in alarm. She thinks he shouts, calls for the kraken to stop, but then she is once again submerged in the darkness of the Styx, and all she knows is the muffled sound of water rushing past her, until she is airborne.

She lands unceremoniously on the deck of the *Danse Macabre*, flat on her back while clutching her glasses in one hand and a broken silver chain in the other.

Penelope gets to Frankie first, grabbing her slim shoulders and pulling her into something resembling a hug. When she leans back, her eyes rove over Frankie and her rumpled, wet appearance.

"I thought—we all thought you were lost. What's that?"

"A necklace," she says, dazedly. "I was—"

Frankie is interrupted by a tap on her shoulder, and she blinks at the large tentacle hovering above her. It unfurls, dropping a small book right into Frankie's lap.

Frankie squints out into the veil of rain at the one shiny eye just above the surface. She raises a hand and says, "Thank you," though it becomes more of a question than she intends. Her mind is still spinning with the past few minutes. Hours? Seconds? She has no idea how long she was in the river. If it wasn't for the necklace in her hand, she would think it had all been a hallucination.

The kraken blinks twice. Frankie decides to interpret this as "You're welcome." The creature slips silently beneath the waves.

Frankie looks down at the book. She fingers the corner, seemingly unable to comprehend what she's holding. It's Penelope who says the words though, hand gripping Frankie's shoulder almost painfully.

"It's Beau's passport."

The passengers aboard the *Danse Macabre* once again retire to their rooms, an unspoken agreement to only resurface at dinner time hanging over their heads.

With a killer on board and a failed plan to request help, spirits are low, inching toward ill-natured and irritable. Mrs. Brightly snaps at Alistair as he offers to help her down the stairs, and Matilda is shaking so badly, the tea sloshes over the sides of her cup as she makes her way back to her cabin. The captain seems to be unaware that his nervous muttering, punctuated with a hiss every few seconds, is no longer just inside of his head.

The rain continues its pattern against the boat, as the anxiety of staying moored for so long crescendos and they part ways with some relief.

Penelope leads Frankie to Cabin Five with a protective arm around her shoulders. She sits primly on the edge of the bed while Frankie changes into dry clothing. After being outside on the observation deck, Penelope's clothing is soaked through, as well, and her teeth chatter against the cold. When Frankie tosses her an oversized night-shirt and a spare coat, Penelope doesn't think twice about changing into it. Even though she does make a comment on how the color of the coat washes out her complexion, it lacks any particular acidity.

They hang their wet clothes in the bathroom to dry, and Penelope returns to her spot on the edge of the bed.

"Are you sure it was real? Maybe the water has some sort of hallucinogenic effect?" she asks, after listening to Frankie's description of the boy with black eyes.

"Then where did I get this?" Frankie holds up the broken chain, and it sparkles in the low light of the room.

Penelope grabs the necklace from Frankie and holds it up to the lamp. The chain itself is quite mundane, and the charm on it is just a simple round pendant—but the symbol carved on the pendant is what makes Penelope shiver. The carving looks like a snake, and if she stares at it for too long, it almost looks as if it's moving. She gratefully hands it back to Frankie. "So, you were under the river?"

Frankie turns her head to the side, squeezing her hair with a towel. "Maybe. I don't know. I couldn't tell which way was up, but if the *Danse Macabre* is up, then I must have gone down."

"If Beau fell overboard, do you think he went to the same place?"

Frankie lifts a shoulder. "I don't know. I wish the kraken hadn't pulled me out so quickly."

"And what did the man say again?"

"Something like, 'How did you get here?'"

"He seemed startled?"

Frankie nods.

Penelope sits down on the bed again, fingering

the corner of the water-soaked passport. "So, would you say it seemed like he wasn't expecting anyone to pop in unannounced like that?"

Frankie wanders back into the bathroom, and her voice echoes against the tiled walls when she answers. "I suppose so. It all happened so fast." She leans against the doorframe, arms folded. "What are you thinking?"

"I'm thinking that if he was so startled, you might have been the first person to show up the way you did."

"Meaning it's unlikely Beau traveled to the same place," Frankie adds, despondently. She disappears into the bathroom again.

Penelope stares at the passport as if Beau will suddenly walk out of its water-soaked pages. A cold, slimy fear steals through her.

This is why, as Frankie comes out of the bathroom again, Penelope musters the strength to say her fears out loud. Her throat is dry and the words come out as a croak. She clears her throat and tries again. "What happens when you die in Death without a passport?"

Frankie is so silent, Penelope wonders if she heard her. She looks up to repeat herself, but finds Frankie staring straight at her, chewing her lower lip in thought.

"I don't know," she replies eventually, with a shake of her head.

"And we're sure the kraken didn't eat him?"

"Why would she return the passport if she was responsible for his death?"

Penelope lifts a shoulder as she tugs the coat tight around herself, fingering the edge of a frayed cuff. Despite the fact that it is totally the wrong color for her, she is grateful for the comfort of silk linings and waxed canvas. Fabrics, patterns, and threads have an order—a predictability—to them that her personal existence is sorely lacking at the present moment. Her fingers itch to embroider something, or move a chess piece across a board, or write a list. Organize a bookshelf by author's last name.

Color-code her day planner. Catalog the number of light bulbs on board. Inventory the bar stock.

Anything other than waiting for a storm to pass.

A storm that can't pass until she calms down, she reminds herself. She's certain of that fact now, as she thinks about lightning and hears the corresponding crack outside. It feels tethered to her soul, an extension of herself.

"I think it's me," she says.

Frankie is cleaning her glasses with a silk cloth. "What?" She holds the glasses up to her face and scowls at a particularly stubborn fleck of dust. She continues cleaning.

"The storm. I think it's me doing it."

Frankie arches an eyebrow as she adjusts her glasses. She plops down on the bed, nearly dislodging Penelope from the edge. With a pointed look, Penelope stands, smooths the t-shirt, then sits down gracefully, leaning against the headboard with legs outstretched. Frankie does the same but can't seem to sit still, uncrossing and crossing her legs again. Penelope's legs are long and smooth, particularly when compared to Frankie's, which are pale and veiny. Penelope wonders where the scar on her knee came from. Was it from the infamous bike dare that Beau told her about once? Penelope bets that Frankie was the type of kid who wasn't afraid to fall.

Penelope has no such scars. Falling was failing, and Penelope Church wasn't allowed to fail.

Frankie shifts again and pulls the quilt over her legs. "A little chilly," she says, with a thin smile. "Why do you think the storm is your fault?" she asks, not unkindly.

Penelope explains about the lightning she conjured at the Next Step offices and how it led to her special issuance passport. "I thought it was a fluke, but it happens sometimes, when I'm annoyed or upset. I think that's what's happening now."

As Frankie listens, her eyebrows knit together. "The rain did start after we realized Beau was gone. It could definitely be tied to your emotions.

Weather-shifting is almost always an emotional thing. Do you think you can turn off the rain? Now that you know you're the one causing it?"

"I don't know." Penelope shrugs, tugging the coat around herself. She's starting to understand why Frankie wears it. It's warm and comforting—a bit like a hug. "I don't know how to. I'm not a witch."

Frankie's glasses reflect the bedside lamp and temporarily hide her eyes as she turns to look at Penelope. "What if you were though?" And then, at Penelope's incredulous eyebrow raise, she adds, "No, hear me out." She places a hand on Penelope's arm. "I know your death is a sore point, and I'm truly sorry for my part in it, but I was doing a simple spell at the time. A ritual to rid myself of feelings that were..." She pauses, lips quirked to the side, "Feelings that were too much for me to carry. I needed to get it off of my chest. What if—and I realize this is a big if—but, what if, those feelings manifested as magic that then latched onto you before you died? It would make sense, if you've gained an emotional type of magic."

"What kind of feelings?"

Frankie blinks. "What?"

"What kind of feelings were you trying to get rid of?"

"Feelings of jealousy," she says quietly. "Jealousy of you. Because I wanted Beau to be my boyfriend, and I turned my anger onto you, not acknowledging that I could have tried harder to keep Beau in my life when we were younger. I mean, I know we were just kids and kids do stupid things, but..." She shakes her head and then lets it fall back against the headboard with a thud. "I could have tried harder to show him that I care about him. Not that that would have changed his feelings for you. You're perfect. I mean, of course. Everyone who meets must be jealous. But at least I wouldn't have had all this pent-up anger if —"

"You do realize that you just tried to tell me that my death was my own fault, right?"

"Oh, I didn't mean—"

"I'm joking. Mostly." Penelope bumps Frankie's shoulder with her own. "If that's true, then what can we do to stop this storm? I've tried my normal breathing exercises, but I'm just so worried and anxious about Beau. I can't relax."

Frankie leans down to pick up her messenger bag. She pulls out a leather-bound book and begins flipping through the pages. "There's a spell we can try." She angles the book toward Penelope and points. "This one. It's mostly meditation and a few Latin incantations. But it's for clear skies and sunny days."

As Penelope reads through the spell, she asks, "Why can't you do the weather spell yourself?"

Frankie adjusts her glasses. "It doesn't work that way. When I died, I lost my magic—the magic I was born with anyway—and gained another type of magic."

She closes the book and hands it back to Frankie. "What kind of magic?"

"I can open doors, move between worlds. I

exist within the broader context of Death, though. I can manipulate what's already dead and whatever is here, in Death proper or even Souls Town to an extent, but I can't create or unmake the dead. I'm bound by the rules of this place. My job description is very specific."

Penelope remembers Beau telling her about Frankie's job and what had to happen in order for her to finish her training. "And it's true that you... that your family sacrificed you?"

"Yes, it's tradition. Passed down from my ancestors so long ago, no one even remembers a time when we didn't pick someone to be sacrificed."

"That's..."

"Morbid? Weird? Appallingly useless?"

"Sad," she says. "Barbaric," she adds, with a flash of fierceness that makes Frankie's stomach flip. "Do you enjoy it at least?"

"No, but maybe that's because I'm terrible at it. Anyway, I've had eighteen years to come to terms with my fate. You didn't even have that." An awkward pause. "I am sorry, you know."

Penelope shrugs. "What's done is done. No use crying over spilled ectoplasm."

"Or mango martini."

Penelope shudders. "That was unfortunate. I hate that I can't change what I'm wearing in Life. I'm stuck with that terrible stained dress for all of eternity."

The reminder of Life brings them back to Beau, and the sound of the rain outside seems louder all of a sudden. Neither of them says it, but they are both thinking it: if Beau is indeed dead, Penelope won't have to worry about her outfit in Life at all. Beau was the only thing keeping her tethered to that realm.

Penelope knows that Beau was the only thing keeping Frankie tethered to that realm, too.

They both drift off with their own thoughts for a moment as the silence turns from companionable to awkward.

Frankie fiddles with the stolen necklace,

passing her thumb over the snake symbol.

"What are you thinking?" asks Penelope.

"It feels funny. The symbol."

"Like it's moving."

Frankie nods. "I suppose I should try to return it, huh?" Her frown deepens, and she stuffs the necklace into the front pocket of her coat.

"One thing at a time," says Penelope. "Do you think we should let the others know? About the weather spell?"

Frankie glances down, tucking the quilt in under her legs. "I think we should probably keep the magic thing to ourselves. It's rare to have such power and I wouldn't want..." She finally looks up at Penelope. "I would just worry that someone would try to..." She lets the sentence fall, unsure of how to continue.

"People are terrible and evil even in Death?" Penelope guesses.

"Especially in Death." A bell sounds from the dining room, letting the passengers know that dinner is about to be served. "I guess we should head upstairs."

"I'm just going to stop by my cabin before dinner and, um," Penelope glances down at the t-shirt and coat. "Change into something more appropriate."

It is only a few minutes later when Penelope, back in her cabin and sorting through her clothing, realizes what Frankie has unknowingly given them both: *leverage*.

CHAPTER 12

FALSE EGG

Wool, waxed canvas, silk. Frankie has many coats stuffed in her messenger bag, almost all of them hand-me-downs from Hart witches of the past. Regardless of their construction and history, they have one thing in common: they are refreshingly lacking in style.

She likes that they are big and bulky and hide her diminutive size. When she was alive, she was proud of her fashion choices, seeing herself as a necessary counterpoint to her glossy-lipped, artificially-tanned peers with their low-slung jeans and short, barely-there skirts.

Not that there's anything wrong with that style of dressing. Frankie thinks all people should be free to wear whatever they want. Her issue lies more with the assumption that she should dress a certain way because of her gender; that is the principle from which she is rebelling.

Penelope always fell somewhere in between Frankie and the other girls in their class. While she wore the same articles of clothing, she did so in moderation, like pairing short skirts with modest blouses. She balanced grungy with feminine, dressy with casual. She was a fashion icon at school and, somehow, even in Death, she remains the same. Beau told her once that Penelope hopes to become a personal stylist, which, she admits, is a fitting career path for her.

Of course, when Penelope is late to dinner, Frankie half-expects the reason to be her inability to make a decision regarding tonight's attire. They've been on this boat for much longer than intended, and surely, even the fashion icon that she is, she must be running out of clothing choices? Penelope, after all, does not have access to her own personal pocket universe.

And yet, when she saunters into the dining room, Frankie is struck with the realization that Penelope, for all her faults, knows how to wear just about anything, including the baggy, frayed coat that Frankie had given her earlier—so much so that Frankie wonders if it's not the coat that is unstylish, but actually herself.

Penelope's black mini skirt, fitted t-shirt, chunky-soled platform heels are highlighted along with the open coat, sleeves rolled up to her elbows in a casual slouch that turns the outfit from preppy to whimsical in a way Frankie knows she herself would never be able to replicate, even with the same exact clothing.

Frankie raises an eyebrow. "Is that my shirt? What did you do to it?"

Penelope blinks, eyes wide. "Nothing. It's called styling."

"But…it looks so different."

"Well, I think you look lovely dear," says Matilda.

"Yes, just lovely," chimes Mrs. Brightly with a hint of impatience. "Now that we all agree, perhaps we could eat?"

Frankie chooses to think that Mrs. Brightly's tone is a side effect of the general feeling of fatigue that permeates the room. They are all feeling as dreary as the view outside the windows, as the strain of enclosed spaces and the threat of another attack looms over all of them. Although no one has said much, they are all thinking the same thing: any one of them could be next.

The captain stands and clinks his fork against his glass to gather everyone's attention. "Now, I know this trip has had some, er, setbacks, but I hope you won't let any of that influence your reviews. There is an exit survey—"

Penelope nearly chokes on her champagne. She sits her glass down with a thunk. "An exit survey?

Are you kidding me? You're worried about reviews when one of your passengers is missing, presumed dead and possibly murdered, and another has been viciously attacked, all the while, we are moored in the middle of nowhere while we wait for a potentially dangerous storm to pass?"

Silence follows Penelope's interruption, so loud Frankie can hear ringing in her ears. Outside, the storm is picking up strength again. Frankie places her hand on Penelope's arm. "You need to calm down," she says behind gritted teeth.

"He's trying his best, dearie," says Matilda. "And anyway, there's no proof that Beau was mur—"

"Is he?" Penelope's look is particularly scathing. "Seems to me like our esteemed captain is sitting around twiddling his thumbs—"

"I don't have thumbs."

"It's a figure of speech." Penelope levels her gaze at the captain, leaning in closer. "Seems to me that anyone who pretends to be drunk half the time is trying to get us to look the other way, leaving him free to go around murdering his passengers."

There is a shocked gasp, but Penelope's eyes stay narrowed at the alligator, whose mouth is opening and snapping shut with indignation. Frankie tugs on the coat sleeve again, and Penelope angles her head toward her, yet keeps her eyes on the captain. "Penelope, what exactly is the end game here?" she hisses.

"I'm not sure," she whispers back, her gaze flicking to Frankie for a brief moment. "I just...I don't know." She slumps backward, and addresses the room. "I'm sorry. I don't know what's wrong with me."

Frankie pinches her lips together. She has the distinct impression that Penelope's outfit and expertly applied makeup are a bit like armor for her; that when she walked into the dining room and drew the eyes of everyone present, she was walking into battle. Frankie wears her coat similarly, only it's to hide rather than to be seen.

For a moment, Frankie realizes that she and

Penelope are not so different from one another. It's utterly cliché to be bonded together over a boy (regardless of one's feelings for said boy) and Frankie thinks there's more to this tenuous connection between her and Penelope. Are they becoming friends? No, not quite, she thinks. *Investigative partners* feels more accurate.

There is a fleeting moment where the investigative partners make eye contact, and Frankie just catches the sly wink from Penelope. Then, Penelope blinks, eyes watery with unshed tears, and with a sob, she begins to cry.

Penelope is also quite good at causing a spectacle, too, Frankie thinks, watching as her lower lip quivers. Her hand shakes as she wipes a tear from her cheek. "Someone hurt Beau. I think we can all agree on that. And I think it would be best if we cleared the air."

"I think that sounds reasonable," says Frankie, glancing around the room.

Penelope leans across Frankie, pointing a finger

at Matilda. "What exactly are you transporting and why did you kill Beau?"

"I don't have to answer that."

"Listen, Frankie and I have the power to stop this storm and get us home." As if to prove her point, a crack of lightning sounds above them, much closer than any previous strikes. It fizzles against the roof, trickling down the windows in a shower of blue sparks. The lights flicker. "But we're not going to do that until we get some answers."

Frankie nods. "Answer the questions. We get out of this storm and back on a solid branch."

Matilda seems to cast about for what to say next. Her gaze shifts, almost imperceptibly, toward the captain, whose own attention is staunchly aimed at a spot just above Penelope's right shoulder.

"I can't tell you what I'm transporting," Matilda says at length, "but I can tell you that it has nothing to do with what happened to Beau, and I certainly don't have anything against Alistair. But..." Matilda straightens her shoulders in the midst of a personal pep talk. "But I can show you, if it will put your minds at ease."

"Matilda, you can't—" begins Captain Jasper.

Matilda is not deterred. She raises her voice over the captain's protestations. "I must have everyone's word that you will not share what I'm about to show you all."

In a trice, it seems, they all acquiesce to keep their silence ("What happens on the Styx, stays on the Styx," warns Captain Jasper), and Matilda leaves to retrieve her package from the unoccupied Cabin Six, where it's been safe under the bed. When she appears a moment later, she's carrying a wooden crate that she places gently on the table.

With one last look at Captain Jasper, she opens the lid to reveal a velvet lined interior. Nestled inside is an egg, milky-white with brown speckles, entirely unassuming if it weren't for its size, which is larger than the chicken eggs to which Frankie is accustomed. Frankie reckons it's about the size of her hand, if she were to stretch her fingers out as wide as they can go. The coloring is mundane, but the size is what makes Frankie think it's a mythical creature.

She corrects herself: magical, not mythical. It's certainly not a dragon egg—they tend to come in jewel tones, or even occasionally, actual metals. Perhaps a basilisk? But she once read that their eggs are made of limestone and alabaster—not this delicate semipermeable calcium carbonate membrane. A giant chicken? Do those exist?

Frankie chances a look at Penelope who is staring intently at the egg, fingers clenched like a child at a museum, itching to touch the art.

"It's a wyvern egg," says Captain Jasper.

Frankie looks up, startled. "But wyverns have been extinct for centuries. They were hunted to extinction, in fact, by vampires. The last known sighting was in..."

"The sixteenth century," says Matilda.

Five pairs of eyes suddenly swerve toward Alistair. He grimaces. "Yes, my brethren do appreciate a variety of blood types. But I wasn't alive then. And anyway, I never took part in the more adventurous eating habits of my contemporaries."

"There's only a handful left," continues Matilda. "This particular egg, however, is destined to go to a private buyer—someone who collects rare creatures, but only to eventually eat them." As Matilda speaks, her voice turns hard with anger. "They treat the poor things terribly in the meantime. I just couldn't stand by and—and—let them suffer." Matilda is momentarily at a loss for words as she grapples with her frustration and anger at the unnamed private buyers. She slumps into a vacant chair. Captain Jasper pats her shoulder. She looks up at him gratefully, and he takes this as a cue to continue for her.

"I work with a magical beast rescue and sanctuary from time to time," he says. "Sailing the river, we do occasionally come across injured creatures, or even just creatures who need a safe space to heal from some trauma." He looks down at the egg. "When Matilda told me about her clients—the things she was forced to be complicit in—well, we decided to enact a plan to get the eggs to the sanctuary, where they can hatch and be safe to live a full, happy life. This is the third time we've made this trip. The first two were tricky, because I was in charge of a high-capacity ferry and there were too many people about."

"Very risky," interjects Matilda, with a somber shake of her head.

"Yes, too risky. So, when the *Danse Macabre* position came up, I decided to take it. Fewer passengers, less oversight."

"And why do you pretend to be drunk? I know that's not alcohol in that flask you keep sneaking sips from."

Captain Jasper frowns, as much as an alligator is capable of doing so at least. "I'm not pretending to be drunk. I do have an alcohol-based tincture in my flask, but it's medicinal. Valerian root—meant to calm the nerves. Lives are at stake here, after all."

They all glance back down at the life at stake, the egg, nestled in its velvet cradle.

"I had to pretend to be late for the *Stygian Jewel*," continues Matilda, after a fortifying sip of tea. "Because there's no way that the company I work for would pay for a ticket at this price."

Penelope tears her gaze from the wyvern egg. "So what's the plan, exactly? As soon as you show up without the egg, your client will know what you've done."

Matilda gives Penelope a shaky smile and lifts the velvet lining, which is affixed to a removable foam cradle. Underneath is an egg that is similar in size, but a stony gray, spotted with yellow and green. "We switch the wyvern egg with this fake egg."

"A fake egg won't hatch. What do you tell the clients then?" asks Frankie.

"Because wyvern eggs are so rare, not much is known about them. I always tell the clients beforehand that there is a risk that the egg isn't fertilized correctly and that it might not hatch. But even an unhatched wyvern egg is a rare piece to have in a collection."

"And no one's ever noticed that the wyvern egg isn't even a real egg?" asks Alistair.

"Not so far," says Matilda, sharing a look with the captain.

Frankie reaches out and touches the decoy. The replica is not an exact match, but it makes a fairly convincing egg, she thinks, running her finger along the bumpy shell.

"Smart not to make them look exactly the same," says Penelope, with a nod.

"Oh, that was Jasper's idea."

"Anything we can do to confuse the market," he adds. "Everyone will think wyvern eggs look like this, so if a legitimate one shows up, no one will believe it."

Frankie frowns. "But Beau saw the corner of the package. He thought you were smuggling something illegal."

"Oh, certainly not illegal. But not exactly legal either," admits Matilda. "Besides, all he saw was the logo for the company I work for. See?" She holds up the lid of the box, which shows a skull next to the company name, Skelly's Imports.

Frankie shakes her head. "But Beau said he saw you. The night he disappeared. He said he ran into you in the hallway."

"Yes, I was on my way to talk to Jasper. To go over the plan."

Jasper nods. "We were together the whole night.

"I hate to interrupt," interrupts Alistair, "but something is happening to the egg."

They all glance down at the wyvern egg, shifting slightly in its velvet nest. It seems to glow, a pulsing golden light that quickens in speed until it becomes persistent—a single note vibrating so strongly, Frankie can hear it cutting through the gloom of the storm like a hymn.

Frankie feels the tension in her shoulders loosening as the sound sinks into her skin like sunshine. She looks around the room and sees matching expressions on the other faces, lit up in an otherworldly golden glow. Heaven doesn't exist—there's only one afterlife and she's in it—but if it did, Frankie imagines it would look and sound like this.

Then, the egg cracks, a tiny noise lost against the sound of a surprised roll of thunder, and out from the broken shell tumbles a pale creature, pearlescent scales shimmering against the dark velvet cradle. Their leathery wings stretch outward, and their snake-like body unfurls, with a too-large head that wobbles as the creature looks up at their audience.

The wyvern blinks their large, round eyes and lifts up on two legs, but the weight of their wings and head is unexpected. The tiny beast tumbles forward. Penelope reaches out and cups a hand around the wyvern, to provide support as they attempt to stand again.

"There you go, little one," she says, kneeling down until she is eye-level with the wyvern. The creature lets out a croaky chirp, nuzzling into Penelope's palm.

"I think they like you," says Frankie, a hint of a smile playing on her lips.

"Indeed," says Matilda, curiously. "They've never hatched during transport before. I don't know if that's normal."

"Well, now that we've sorted out this misunderstanding," interjects Alistair. "Could we begin the process to disperse the rain?"

Penelope cradles the wyvern against her chest. "Certainly. Reaper regulations state that Frankie can only use her power for Reaper business. However, our circumstances are quickly becoming an emergency. According to the Reaper handbook, Frankie is allowed to use her powers in the event that she or her client become stranded or are in some sort of distress."

It's a blatant lie, and Frankie arches an eyebrow

at Penelope, who merely lifts a shoulder.

"I have graciously offered my assistance with this task," she continues. "You may not know this, but I have a special issuance passport which affords me certain privileges and I think my skills, combined with Frankie's, will help us out of this mess."

The wyvern chirps.

"Yes, you can help too, Little One," says Penelope, using the tip of her finger to pet the wyvern's scaly head. Little One leans into the touch, leg jumping up and down in appreciation.

The rain lashes at the window and the boat wobbles, waves sloshing up and over the observation deck, slipping under the small gap between the balcony doors and the dining room floor. It seeps into the rug, and Penelope can smell the salty, sulfurous odor of the river water.

"Just relax," Frankie says.

As if it's easy to do when she can feel the eyes of the other passengers, like hot needles piercing her back.

She and Frankie are sitting on the floor, legs crossed and knees just touching, while everyone else watches them eagerly. She had been hoping she would have had time to at least learn her lines, but after Matilda's confession, everything seemed to move so quickly. The book was retrieved. A space on the floor cleared so that they could begin the meditation.

The wyvern, now taken to the name Little One, is nestled in the crook between Penelope's neck and shoulder, using her hair as a blanket. Little One lets out a chirp.

"I'm trying," she tells Little One. She looks at Frankie. "I really am."

Frankie's expression is oddly serene and carefree. Penelope can't help but feel their roles are reversed. Then again, magic is something Frankie knows more about. If they were discussing fabric bias or the benefits of an A-line silhouette, then perhaps Penelope wouldn't feel so nervous.

"What could go wrong?" Frankie asks.

It's quite disarming to have her own words used on her—disarming, but effective. "We could fail."

"And what happens then?"

"We try again."

Frankie smirks. "You can do this, Penelope Church." The smirk widens into a smile. "I trust you."

Little One chirps their agreement.

In any other situation, Penelope would question Frankie's confidence, maybe even mistake it for sarcasm. But the glint in Frankie's eye startles Penelope out of old habits. She has the sudden urge to smile, her chest tight with a feeling she can't quite define.

"Right. Okay. Yes. Let's do this." She grabs Frankie's hands.

Little One bumps Penelope's neck with the top of their head, creating a small spark of magic that travels down her arm. She feels a flush of gratitude for the tiny creature, who feels warm against her skin. It's true that Little One seems inordinately attached to her, even though they've been hatched for less than an hour. Penelope feels a little attached as well, already worried for the tiny creature and the myriad ways they could be injured in this great, big, scary world.

Penelope holds onto the warmth. As she lets her mind quiet, focusing only on the feeling of her hands intertwined with Frankie's and the warmth of Little One against her neck, she becomes aware of what she can only assume is the spirit of the people around her.

Little One is all gold, white-bright light. Sunshine, she supposes. Frankie is a jumble of thorny vines, but dotted with porcelain white blooms and rooted in freshly turned soil. She is all moonlight and softly hooting owls.

Alistair is circled in dark hues and shadows tinged with crimson stains, but with a hint of jasmine and sea salt. Matilda is green, fresh dew-drenched grass and the smell of rain in the forest mingling with a cup of black tea. Captain Jasper is a sound, the squeal of mosquitoes, the call of toads at night, the gentle lapping of water against clay and earth.

And Penelope herself? She is stardust, swirling in the dark, forming whatever her mind conjures, dispersing, and forming again into something new.

As Frankie explained, the weather spell is simple because it relies on feelings and not complicated arrangements of words or actions. There is just one activating phrase, a handful of foreign words (Latin twisted with other languages to form what Frankie called "the witch's tongue").

Penelope reads the phrase, her voice melding with Frankie's. As their tongues stumble slightly over the foreign sounds, Penelope feels a spark of magic in her fingertips that reminds her of soft, silky petals. She wonders if Frankie has some left-over mischief she doesn't know about. At the very least, Penelope doesn't feel alone in casting the spell, with Frankie's spirit and Little One's warmth. The trio's magic melds together into a seamless flow of mischief.

They repeat the phrase, and Penelope thinks about the cool rain against her cheeks, followed by the thought of the absence of rain.

She licks her lips, imagines the taste of water, metallic and sulfurous, and then envisions the steam as the rain drops burn away with the magic of her words; she wishes for still waters, for cloudless skies, for stars that sparkle like jewels, like Little One's eyes, bright and shimmering with marvelous scrutiny.

It takes some moments for Penelope to realize that the notes of her voice are once again singular, a thin, untrained soprano. She stops abruptly, and her eyes fly open.

Frankie is smiling. "Hear that? It's silent. No more rain."

Penelope unfolds herself from the floor and

makes her way onto the observation deck. She feels the others following her, but pays them no mind as she takes in the cool, crisp air, and the placid expanse of the Styx, stretching beyond into a green-tinged horizon. The stars seem to awaken one-by-one, and Penelope can almost hear them yawning after their slumber.

"What's that?" asks Mrs. Brightly, coming to grasp the railing. "Out there?" She points toward the horizon, which is broken only by a dark shape swiftly approaching.

"It's a boat," says Alistair, standing next to Mrs. Brightly. "They're heading for us."

"A rescue boat?" asks Matilda, worrying her bottom lip. "They got our letter?" She glances nervously at the wyvern. "Perhaps we should hide—" She reaches for the Little One, but Little One snaps at her fingers.

"It's too late, now," says the Captain, with a desolate shrug as the boat sidles up beside them. They can see the crew, three of them including the captain at the helm, and the big red letters painted on the side that pronounce the vessel as *River Guard 7.*

CHAPTER 13

PRECINCT 666

The walrus who boards the *Danse Macabre* is rather stern, his countenance made sterner by his beady eyes and large tusks that protrude out on either side of his thick, sandy-colored mustache.

The new arrival hasn't said anything, but the mustache moves as if it has a mind of its own, itching to say something.

Surprisingly, the majority of the new arrival's appearance is decidedly less walrus-like, and he strides forward on short, stubby legs, arms akimbo as he stuffs his webbed hands in the tiny pockets on his coat.

The coat is the standard River Guard uniform, crisp white wool with navy blue shoulder boards embroidered with silver bars. The pin on his chest marks him as an Admiral. His boots echo ominously against the rain slicked deck of the *Danse Macabre* and the sound reminds Frankie of the thunder they have just tamed.

"Well," says the walrus. Frankie squints and reads his name tag.

Admiral Barnaby Kensington

First Tributary, River Guard

Admiral Kensington pauses, his mustache wiggly up and down. "Earlier today, I received a message requiring the urgent presence of the River Guard to help a stranded vessel and its passengers. We arrived at the provided coordinates only to find ourselves confronted with an impenetrable veil of rain." The mustache twitches right to left. "Shortly after our arrival, the rain clears and we are able to locate the vessel in distress." He sweeps his arm to encompass the boat and the passengers standing in front of him. "Imagine our surprise that we've found the lost *Danse Macabre* and yet, it would seem that you are not exactly in distress." He pauses again, his eyes wide as if waiting for the answer to his unasked question. "Well, what's the meaning of all of this?" And then he adds, in response to their blank faces, "Who's in charge?"

The passengers step backwards, leaving Penelope and Frankie standing in front. Frankie rolls her eyes but steps forward, arms crossed. "There was a storm. But it's cleared up now, Admiral Kensington."

"If you're here to rescue us," adds Penelope, inspecting her fingernails, "you're too late."

Admiral Kensington doesn't seem to know how to respond. The mustache squirms erratically. "Well—I—you—who are you?"

"I'm Penelope Church. And if you're finished—"

"Now hold on a minute," says Admiral Kensington, hand raised. "Storms don't just happen. I need to know how and why such an event occurred.

If there's been any illegal use of an artifact or—"

"Nothing illegal here," interjects Matilda, wringing her hands. She glances at Penelope's shoulder.

Admiral Kensington follows her gaze to Little One, who is still perched on Penelope's shoulder, though at least partially hidden by the curtain of her hair. "What is that?"

"It's a chicken," says Frankie, moving to stand in front of Penelope, arms folded authoritatively. "Just hatched, which is why it looks a little funny. Now, you're an Admiral in the River Guard, and it is my duty as a Reaper to inform you that at least two crimes have been committed on this boat and the storm was not one of them." Frankie places a hand on his arm and begins to lead him back toward *River Guard 7*.

"That may be, uh—what is your name?" asks the admiral.

"Reaper Hart."

"Crimes may have been committed, but let's

leave it to the professionals to determine what they are. Which is to say, leave it to me to determine. Now," he says, extracting himself from Frankie's grip, "I must insist, Reaper Hart, on some explanations as to what caused the storm. And I must insist on seeing some identification. For everyone here."

"And what if we don't comply with your insistence?" asks Penelope.

"Then we can take this conversation down to the station."

The light clicks on, and Frankie blinks against the sudden change. She blocks the sudden intrusion with her hand. "Is this really necessary?"

The interrogation room is a droll gray cinder block square with a too-bright bare bulb hanging from a cord in the middle of the room. It smells of damp and green things, and although shadows reside heavily in the corners of the room, Frankie wouldn't be surprised if mold was growing expeditiously. In all, a dungeon would feel homier. Of course, what should one expect when being interrogated at Precinct 666?

When Admiral Kensington told them where he was transferring them, Frankie smirked incredulously. "It's just a coincidence," he said adamantly, but perhaps a little too quickly; Frankie is disinclined to believe him.

Beside her, Penelope folds her arms across her chest. "It isn't. Something unusual happened, and he's worried that the higher-ups will pin it all on him if he lets a suspected criminal go. But he doesn't even know what the crime is."

Frankie raises her eyebrow. "Did we do something illegal? I didn't realize that being caught in a storm was against the law. Like I said earlier, two crimes. The storm was not one of them."

Penelope leans forward, her voice hardening with frustration. "We didn't do anything illegal. But someone did and I demand justice!" She slaps the tabletop with an open palm as added punctuation.

Little One, nestled in the front pocket of Penelope's coat, pops their head up to chirp in agreement and then slips back down. Frankie clears her throat.

"Too much?" Penelope asks, *sotto voce.*

"A bit," admits Frankie with a shrug.

"Look," says the Admiral, straightening a stack of papers in front of him. The mustache twitches as he thumbs through Penelope's passport. He lets it drop back onto the scuffed wood tabletop. "Ms. Church, I'll be honest with you. This whole thing is a mess. The sooner we get to the bottom of things, the sooner you and—" He glances at Frankie's Reaper credentials. The slim leather wallet lies open on the table, and the badge looks shiny and new. "You and Reaper Hart can be on your merry way." The mustache jumps. "Now, I'm sure you both understand the gravity of the situation."

Frankie smiles, but there is no warmth in the expression. "Explain it to me like I died yesterday, please."

"The storm. It's an anomaly. And it's got everyone quite worried about what it means."

"In a literal or metaphorical sense of the word?" asks Penelope. "Because, literally, a storm is defined as a violent short-lived weather disturbance with lightning, thunder, dense clouds, heavy rain or hail, and strong gusty winds. But metaphorically?" She shrugs. "Probably nothing."

"The storm isn't what's important," says Frankie. "It's the fact that someone got on that boat and yet didn't get off."

"Ah yes," says the admiral, happy to move onto something more familiar. He reads the name from the *Danse Macabre*'s passenger manifest. "Beauregard Astor. Yes, I had a few questions about him."

"As do we," says Penelope. "Like, what are you going to do about apprehending the person who killed him?"

"There was another incident, as well," points out Frankie. "Another passenger was assaulted and we think it's the same perpetrator."

Admiral Kensington is skeptical. "There's no proof that Mr. Astor was killed, for one. And two, you're assuming the two events are linked."

"Coincidences are rare. I think it's best to work on the assumption that they are connected," says Penelope dismissively.

"Be that as it may—"

Frankie stops hearing Admiral Kensington's voice as something—a niggling thought—connects in her brain, a proverbial light bulb blinking into existence.

"You should talk to Mrs. Brightly," she says suddenly. "We've ruled out Matilda. Captain Jasper is her alibi, and she's his alibi. I suppose Alistair could have killed Beau, and then injured himself to throw suspicion away from him. But you're right, Pen, the simplest explanation is the most likely. If we have valid reasons to rule out three of the passengers, then the fourth is the murderer." She glances at Penelope, adjusting her glasses with the knuckle of her right index finger, her cheeks flushed with the overly-familiar, subconscious shortening of Penelope's name. Feeling a little helpless in the silence that follows, she adds, "Right?"

Penelope gives her an unreadable sideways look. "Yes, Frank. You're right." Then, to Admiral Kensington, "You are going to question her, aren't you?"

"Of course." He slides their credentials back toward them, waving a webbed hand dismissively. "She's next on my list."

Before the admiral leaves, Frankie calls out after him. "Might I suggest filing an information request with the Life Liaison Office before you speak with her?"

Mrs. Brightly sits in Interrogation Room Five. The bare bulb hanging from a chain in the center of the room casts thick shadows across her face. The dark shape of her figure stretches grotesquely against the stone wall behind her. She smiles politely at the stern, uniformed guard standing by the door, but the polite smile slides away as Frankie walks into the room. "Oh, it's you again."

"Yes, it's me. Your assigned Reaper, who, in cases like this, may act as a legal representative."

"Legal representative?" Her eyes bulge slightly at the implication. "Why would I need legal representation?"

"Because," says Admiral Kensington, entering the room and taking a seat in front of Mrs. Brightly. He places a file folder on the table, hands resting on either side of it. "You murdered Alistair Finch."

"I beg your pardon—"

"Mrs. Brightly." Frankie sits down beside her and places a hand, just briefly, on her shoulder. "We've requisitioned your death certificate and some case files associated with your time in Life."

Frankie nods at Admiral Kensington, who opens the folder and swivels it around so that Mrs. Brightly can read its contents.

"These documents link you with a murder that happened just half an hour before you died." Frankie shifts the papers, until she finds a forensic analysis report, still warm from the printer. "This says that they found your DNA at the crime scene, where Alistair—our Alistair—was found murdered."

Mrs. Brightly reaches out to touch the paper with shaking fingers, though she snatches her hand back before making contact, fingers curling into a fist. "He's not my Alistair," she says, her voice toneless and flat.

"These documents prove that you have a connection with Alistair, and I don't think it's too presumptuous to say that you're behind the attack on him, in both Life and Death. I think you stabbed him while we were on the *Danse Macabre*. I also believe that Alistair's attack and Beau's murder were done by the same culprit." Frankie leans a little closer, trying to catch Mrs. Brightly's eye, yet her gaze is resolutely on her lap, fists still clenched. Her fingers are white and spindly. They look like bones. "But what we don't know from the report is why you killed Alistair in Life and why you killed Beau in Death."

There is a suspended moment of anticipation. Frankie has no idea what Mrs. Brightly is going to say or how she will react to these accusations.

Then, quite suddenly, Mrs. Brightly seems to lose her resolve. She collapses, head bowed under more than just the weight of her eighty-three years. "I bet he doesn't even remember her name," she mumbles.

When she looks up, there are tears in her eyes, white streaks that spill down her cheeks silently. "The vampire. Alistair. I never meant to hurt your Beau. My eyesight isn't what it used to be, you know, and in the dark, they looked quite the same."

"Same height. Same build," says Frankie encouragingly.

Mrs. Brightly nods. "I grabbed a knife from the dining room and just...stabbed him." Mrs. Brightly looks down at her hands, still clenched into tight fists, but Frankie has a feeling she isn't seeing the wrinkled, sun-spotted fingers, but something else. She is lost in her memories, quite unseeing. "My mother was beautiful. Everyone said so. And perhaps that's why Alistair took a liking to her in the first place. She was trusting. Too trusting. She let him into our lives and she paid for it with her blood.

"He killed my father. Then he killed my mother. Then he left. It took me years, my whole life really, to find him, to track him down. And when I did, do you know what I found?" She laughs icily. "I found a gentleman living in comfort. I found a monster masquerading as a man. As a friend, as a valuable member of society. I hated him even more after that." Her voice has turned to acid, the anger so corrosive Frankie can't help but imagine that it's rotting the air as she speaks.

Frankie picks up where Mrs. Brightly leaves off. "So, you kill him. And then you end up in Death, only to be confronted with him again. You must have felt so, so angry."

She nods quickly, jerkily. "Yes. Very angry. The injustice of it all. That me and that—that evil monster. That we would end up on the same boat. A luxury cruise ship! What has he done to earn that?"

Frankie treats this like a rhetorical question. She gently presses Mrs. Brightly to continue. "What happened to Beau after you stabbed him?"

"I don't know. He just disappeared." Mrs. Brightly looks between Frankie, blinking behind her large glasses, and the admiral, looking piercingly at her over his thick facial adornment. Bereft of her anger, she looks deflated. Lost. "What happens now? Am I being arrested?"

"That remains to be seen," admits Admiral Kensington. "Mr. Finch hasn't yet decided to press charges—"

Mrs. Brightly scrunches her nose, as if she smells something particularly foul. "You mean, my fate is dependent upon whether a murderer wants justice?"

Admiral Kensington's mustache twitches as he

attempts to find the correct arrangement of consolatory words, but his efforts are in vain.

Mrs. Brightly's expression deepens. For a moment, Frankie has the impression that she is folding in on herself, her wrinkles becoming more pronounced, the pallor of her skin turning a sickly green. Her eyes begin to yellow around the edges and when she lunges forward, hateful, spiteful words spewing forth with spittle, her clenched, bone-white fingers uncurl from a fist, and she reaches out to grab the admiral with nails sharpened into fine points.

The uniformed guard works quickly to restrain her, gripping her arms behind her back as he expertly slaps iron chains around her wrists.

CHAPTER 14

FOR WHOM THE BELL DID NOT TOLL

Outside in the hall, Penelope looks stonily at the door to the interrogation room, behind which Mrs. Brightly is being questioned.

Her focus is so intent, that it takes her some moments to realize that someone is talking to her. Little One's chirp is what eventually tears her attention away from the door and to the person standing next to her. "What?"

Matilda rolls her eyes in exasperation. "I said, if you'll just let me transport the *chicken* to the *farm* now..." She holds up a small carrier as she darts a look to the office space behind them. "Jasper and I can be on our way."

"What? Oh, right." She glances down at Little One in the front pocket of her coat. "Did you hear that, Little One? You're going to go to a place where you can make friends. Maybe even start a family."

Little One blinks once, then slips back down.

"Come on, Little One. You can't stay with me. I don't know how to take care of you." She tickles the lump in her pocket and Little One squirms. "Little One," she says in a sing-song voice. "Please come out."

Little One pokes their head up again and then pushes themself into the air, their tiny wings beating frantically. They hover in front of Penelope, pearlescent eyes staring intently at her. She has the impression that Little One is trying to tell her something, but she isn't sure what. Then, the wyvern turns around, hisses at Matilda, and settles on Penelope's shoulder with a chirp.

Matilda raises her eyebrows.

"I think Little One wants to stay," says Penelope with a lopsided smile.

"Very well," says Matilda, albeit reluctantly. "Here's my card. Please don't hesitate to call if you ever need assistance with…Little One."

Penelope pockets the card as Matilda walks away, winding her way through the desks and dodging River Guards striding purposefully through the office space. She watches as Matilda has a hushed conversation with Captain Jasper as they leave Precinct 666, the glass door swinging shut behind them.

Penelope turns her attention back to Interrogation Room Five and waits.

When the door opens, it admits a shaken Frankie and a dour admiral. Behind them, Penelope can see Mrs. Brightly, her face twisted and monstrous as she makes an indistinct snarling sound.

"What's happened to her?"

Frankie answers for the admiral. "She became a Vex. A soul that comes to Death with anger inside of them. They're sick. If they don't let go of the anger—or resentment or jealousy or whatever negative emotion—the feeling starts to rot them from the inside out and they turn feral." Frankie gives Penelope a summary of Mrs. Brightly's confession. "She must have been holding onto that resentment and anger for so long. It damaged her soul."

"What happens now? Does she go to jail? A care facility?"

"I'll ask Mr. Finch if he wants to press charges," says Admiral Kensington, "If so, it'll go to a Tribunal and they'll decide her fate. A care facility is most likely for a Vex. As for your friend, Mr. Astor..." He pauses. The mustache twitches left and the right. "That'll be a little harder. If Mr. Astor was to press charges of his own, something might come of it."

Frankie is already shaking her head. "That's the problem. We don't know where he is. Mrs. Brightly said he just disappeared."

"I have his passport," says Penelope. "But we haven't been able to locate him yet."

The mustache puffs out for a second and then is sucked inward as he gives them a less than helpful shrug. "Well, I wish you the best of luck in finding him." Admiral Kensington begins, hurriedly and with some relief, escorting them through the door. "You should check the Next Step offices. See if he's already arrived."

Frankie stops on the threshold, letting Penelope take a few steps down the hallway before she turns back to the admiral. "You said there was a message that we required assistance. Who sent the message?"

"Beats me," he says, mustache quivering. "It just came through on the radio."

"Not a *Danse Macabre* brochure?"

"No, it was a person. Masculine voice. Came in on the emergency channel."

"Thank you," says Frankie, slipping her hands in the pockets of her coat. She nods one last time as the door swings shut behind them.

The lights are just as awful as Penelope remembers, and she is grateful, at least, that her second visit to the Next Step office comes with a change of wardrobe. She is still wearing Frankie's coat, with Little One nestled in the front pocket, and her chunky-soled sandals make her feel stronger and more capable than she probably, in actuality, is.

She's also grateful that she had the wherewithal to pull Frankie into a bathroom before they got here and her lightly-applied concealer makes her feel much more confident. She glances over at Frankie, who had graciously allowed Penelope to add a bit of concealer under her eyes, as well, even as she made snide comments the entire time.

Penelope never spent much time considering Frankie's appearance, beyond the cursory assessment that she lacked style and didn't seem bothered by that fact. If pressed, Penelope would attribute the latter to herself, as well.

But Penelope, in a rare bout of soul-searching, realizes that she is, in fact, quite the opposite. She worries greatly what others think of her, and Frankie—suddenly, remarkably—is no exception to this. The lightly concealed nickname from earlier comes back to Penelope, and she shakes her head at this strange understanding that has blossomed between her and her accidental-murderer. What an afterlife, she thinks mildly. To be working together with Frankie Hart, to care about Frankie's opinions of her.

Beau will find this whole thing entirely amusing.

"Right then," she says, when she realizes that she's been staring a little too long to be polite. Her cheeks flush. "Let's find Beau."

She shoulders her way into the room and makes her way directly to the front desk. Johnsoniela looks up from her keyboard, a bland smile on her lips. Yet when she recognizes Penelope, the smile turns stony. "You! No, I'm not dealing with whatever this is."

"Johnsoniela, please—"

She stands up, hands on her hips. "No," she says again. "I'm taking my lunch break."

Penelope changes tack instantly, as she leans an elbow on the desk and, in a tone of commiseration, says, "Break-ups are hard." Johnsoniela looks warily at her. Penelope can feel Frankie's gaze as well, equally confused. She shakes it off and continues. "Last time I was here, there was an adorable picture of you and someone else." She motions toward the empty spot on the desk, next to the computer. "But it's gone now."

Johnsoniela's lower lip quivers briefly, before she bursts into tears. Penelope springs into action, moving swiftly around the desk to put an arm around Johnsoniela, who, in between hiccups, explains that her boyfriend of two and a half centuries has suddenly left her.

"And he—he told me that—he didn't love me anymore—"

A crisp, cotton handkerchief is presented, fished from the bottom of Frankie's messenger bag. Penelope hands it to Johnsoniela, who wipes at her cheeks while nodding her gratitude. Penelope gives Johnsoniela an indistinct sympathetic noise, as her eyes flit up to Frankie. She angles her head toward the desk, where a leather-bound registry book lies open next to the keyboard.

Frankie shakes her head and mouths, "What?"

Penelope angels her head further, straining her neck as she eyes the open registration book before cutting back to Frankie.

A look of realization dawns on Frankie's face, and she nods, leaning over the desk. With one finger, she pushes the corner of the book so that she can read the list of incoming residents. Penelope turns back to Johnsoniela, murmuring soothing platitudes about what she deserves and assurances that she can do better. Penelope can't see Frankie, but she hears the soft rustle of a page being turned. "He said what to you?" she says to Johnsoniela, a little too loudly.

The receptionist doesn't notice the volume change. "Yes, can you believe that?"

"No," replies Penelope honestly. The more Johnsoniela spills about her former paramour, the more Penelope agrees that she really is better off without him.

Despite her sympathy toward Johnsoniela, Penelope knows she must start extracting herself from the situation. It takes a full five minutes and a promise of a future night out ("Just us girls") to calm her down. They exchange phone numbers, and Penelope says goodbye just as the door swings shut. She waits until they are a few feet away from the office, before pulling Frankie into a small alcove set back from the main hallway.

Frankie smirks. "Maybe you're the one who needs a deerstalker." But the smirk vanishes quickly. "His name wasn't there. I even went back a few pages. Nothing."

"So, he isn't dead?"

"That's what I'm thinking. But there's one more place I want to check, just to make sure."

The row of orange and yellow vinyl seats stretches down the corridor and around the corner. The seats are empty save for the first two, which are occupied by Penelope and Frankie as they wait to be admitted to the Carillon room located in the root levels, in Room -2.

The Carillon is behind the cathedral style doors to Penelope's right. Spreading out from the door is a meticulous arrangement of stone brickwork, heavy enough to dampen the vibration from the billions of bells ringing almost constantly.

"A bell for each death," explains Frankie, repeating the phrase she heard so often during her Reaper training. "Every death is documented, no matter how small."

Penelope looks nervously at the doors. "You've

been here before?”

“Only once, during a tour of the root levels.” It’s mostly true, but Darren had breezed past the Carillon, clopping along dismissively when asked about the intricacies and practicalities of an instrument with billions of bells. He barely explained how to request information from the Carillonneur, saying, “No need. Records are eventually transcribed and sent upstairs.”

“Did a bell ring for me?” asks Penelope, twirling a strand of hair around her finger.

Frankie pushes her glasses further up her nose, then stuffs her hands in her coat pockets before answering. “Of course. One rang for me as well.”

“And I’m assuming there is a record kept of every bell rung?” Frankie confirms with a nod. “So, what are we waiting for? Let’s go in.”

“We’re waiting for that—” Frankie points at the small window in the middle of the door “—to open.”

“And when will it open?”

Frankie lifts a shoulder. “No clue. There’s no set

schedule, at least not that anyone has been able to discern. Records are eventually archived upstairs. Most people decide that waiting for that is easier than getting the attention of the Carillonneur. But it could take up a week for the records to make their way into the database."

"So, we wait for the little window to open?"

"Yep."

A few beats of silence. "Like you and Beau waited for your passports?"

Frankie tries to look at Penelope, but from her angle, she can't fully read the expression on her face, just the straight line of her mouth and her relaxed eyebrows. "Yes, I suppose. Although there was a timer for that."

A few more beats of silence and then, Penelope says, "I think he's in love with you."

Frankie freezes. When she speaks, her voice is foreign to her ears, too small and squeaky. "Why do you say that?"

"It's what we argued about the night he died. I

accused him of...cheating." She whispers the word, as if it's a curse. "He said he loved me, but I refused to believe him. I don't think it was a lie. Just that it wasn't the whole truth. And then he asked me if I wanted him to die for me." She pauses to take a deep, shuddery breath. "And I said yes."

Something hard breaks apart in Frankie's chest. Has Penelope been holding onto this guilt the whole time? Does she think what happened to Beau is because of her words?

"It was Mrs. Brightly who killed Beau. You are not responsible," Frankie says firmly, turning to face Penelope. She prepares herself for what she knows she needs to say next. "And I know Beau loves you. He told me that night, after your fight." She decides to leave out the part where he sat down dejectedly on her bed and told her about his plan to break-up with Penelope when they arrived at their destination.

Instead, she says something worse, the words rushing out together in a semi-coherent string.

"Beau didn't cheat on you. But we kissed. Once. A year ago. Barely a kiss. At my Death Day Party. There was champagne. I threw myself at him. It was me. Not him. He didn't do anything wrong."

Penelope cocks her head to the side, the silky curtain of her hair draping across her shoulder. Her red lips purse in thought. "I know."

"You—what—how?"

"He came home from that party a little drunk. He was mumbling about you as he fell asleep."

"And you didn't say anything?"

She lifts a shoulder. "He seemed regretful. I'm not implying that he regretted kissing you back or anything. But he was trying so hard not to hurt me..." Penelope looks away. "I enjoyed it. For a while at least. He was being so nice and thoughtful." She shakes her head. "It's stupid."

Frankie smiles gently. "I get it. And I hope you know that I would never do something like that again. Especially now that we're...investigative partners."

Penelope grins. "Investigative partners. I like the sound of that. Also, I don't mind a nickname, by the way. But I really hate Pen. Can we come up with something different?"

"Sure...Poppy?"

Penelope grimaces. "We'll workshop it." She glances at the Carillon doors and stands, adjusting her skirt. "I'm sick of waiting." She knocks three times with the side of her fist, the sound echoing down the hallway.

Frankie begins to explain that knocking is futile; because of the sheer cacophony happening behind the doors, an insignificant sound like a knock would only—

The peephole slides open with a click and a gruff voice says, "What's that noise? Who's there?" She can hear the faint sounds of the Carillon in the background, dampened by the reinforced doors.

Frankie shoots up out of her seat, standing on the tips of her toes so she can make eye contact with the person on the other side of the door.

The window is small, and Frankie can only see the person's eyes: slightly slanted, cat-slit pupils set in circles of yellow. She fumbles for her Reaper credentials and then holds the badge up. "We need to speak to the Carillonneur."

"That's me. Name?"

"Frank—"

"Not your name. The person you're looking for."

"Beauregard James Astor the Third," says Penelope hurriedly. She clutches Frankie's shoulder and Frankie can feel her fingers through the stiff fabric of her coat. She understands the tension that's radiating through Penelope's grip.

The Carillonneur's eyes blink once. "Hold." The peephole closes with a click, and Frankie and Penelope are left, once again, waiting silently in the hallway, the anxiety creeping back into their shoulders.

Penelope bounces on the balls of her feet, uncharacteristically chewing on her thumbnail.

Frankie does the opposite, standing as still as possible, gaze narrowed to the window in the door.

When it slides back, the eyes look out, blink once, and then are replaced with a furred hand clutching a small slip of paper. Frankie takes the paper and the window closes again. Penelope reads over Frankie's shoulder.

Name: Beauregard James Astor the Third

Bell Status: Un-rung

Soul Status: [error]

Frankie frowns and knocks on the door. The window slides back and the eyes return. Frankie didn't realize that eyes could look so annoyed without a face to contribute to the expression.

"I'm sorry. I would just like some clarification about the Soul Status. What does error mean?"

The Carillonneur rolls their eyes. "Just that. Error processing Soul Status. Means the status of the soul could not be processed."

The window closes again, the click echoing with a finality that makes Frankie's heart sink.

EPILOGUE

1: A New Branch

Penelope drops a box and looks up, raising an eyebrow at Frankie's single messenger bag. "That's all you have?"

"Yep," she says, flopping down on the couch, recently purchased from a thrift store.

It's a terrible shade of puce, and Penelope has already begun the process of reupholstering it, draping several bolts of fabric across the back. Frankie fingers the edge of a blue velvet. "I like this one."

Penelope quirks her lips to the side, hands on her hips. "Don't you think the green floral would make more of a statement?"

Frankie rolls her eyes. "We'll go with the green floral then."

The studio flat is small, and made even smaller by the wall of boxes labeled *Penelope*. Two matching twin-size beds are pushed up against opposite walls and the couch, along with a scratched second-hand coffee table and a threadbare circular rug are in the middle of the room, facing a large expansive window that shows the river Styx.

They moved in yesterday, and it already feels more like home than her dormitory ever did.

As Penelope begins to unpack her boxes, Frankie picks up her notebook and pen from the coffee table and continues writing her letter of resignation.

"How's the letter going?" Penelope asks, frowning into a box as she looks for something specific. Little One flutters around her in a circle before landing on her shoulder.

Penelope distractedly rubs the top of the wyvern's head as she continues rifling through the box.

"Pretty good." Frankie hands it to Penelope to proof-read.

Dear Director of Reaping,

I would like to tender my resignation effective immediately. Furthermore, I would like to say that it has not been an honor to work with you. The institution that has led to my employment and thereby forced death is barbaric and I, for one, refuse to stand for it any longer.

Unkind regards,

Francesca Hart

Little One gives a chirp of approval.

"And you're sure this is what you want to do?" Penelope asks, uncharacteristically chewing her lower lip.

Frankie nods, folding the paper and slipping it into an envelope. "I was a terrible Reaper. I hated it. Besides, this will give me more time to help with finding Beau."

Penelope's mouth curves into a sad smile, and she reaches out to squeeze Frankie's hand. "I'm worried, Frankie. It's been a week. What if something really bad has happened to him?"

"We'll keep looking," replies Frankie, "no matter how long it takes. I'm sure he's here somewhere."

"Of course," says Penelope with false cheer, returning to her boxes. "Yes," she says more to herself than anything. "We'll find him soon. I'm sure of it."

Frankie can feel her own optimism waning, too. After the Carillon, they made their way to the nearest public library branch. There, they requested maps of every known place in Death, including a detailed map of Souls Town. They've been making their way down a list of potential places Beau could be, ticking them off one by one as their efforts remain fruitless.

The next one on the list is a place called

Elysium, a weird members-only resort from what Frankie has been able to uncover. It can only be reached by a train that follows the flow of one of the sister-rivers. Penelope has already requested two tickets for them to travel there, along with their "service chicken."

Frankie thinks it's unlikely that Beau ended up there, but in the absence of any solid leads, she is grateful that they have a plan, at least.

In her spare time, Penelope has also implemented a letter campaign, writing to various officials listed in the Roots and Branch Directory. She hasn't had any responses so far. However, now that Frankie has resigned, she and Penelope plan to begin the next phase of their plan: plastering the branches with missing posters featuring Beau's picture.

Frankie attaches her letter of resignation to the leg of a carrier-bat and then sends it on its way. As the bat flies off, Frankie feels lighter with one less burden.

Later that night, sleep comes easily for Penelope, but puts up a fight when it gets to Frankie.

She's become accustomed to it. In Life, she slept easily, deeply, *gratefully*. Yet, since she died, she's struggled with insomnia, which seems to be the opposite of most in Death. Almost everyone she knows here can slip into the nothingness of sleep instantly. Penelope is no exception. Frankie can see her sleeping from across the room, long blonde hair hiding her face. Little One is curled up on the pillow, nestled against the crook of her neck.

Frankie snuggles under her quilt. Her mind is restless, filled with churning waves of darkness and messy rooms and black eyes.

There is a part of her that wonders if the strange room under the river was nothing but a hallucination: a side-effect of the black Stygian waters infiltrating her lungs, seeping into her skin.

And yet, the proof that it was real—or at least,

real enough—rests in her palm.

She had initially quite forgotten the necklace, the thing she accidentally stole as the kraken wrenched her back into the waters. Finding it later, after the Carillon, she was startled to realize that the silver isn't cold anymore, but warm with mischief, a spark of electric blue that tingles against her fingers as she rubs the silver medallion.

Since then, she's been slipping her hand into her pocket more frequently, just to feel the spark. To remind herself that it was real and that whoever the man was, he must have been responsible for sending the guard.

Although both she and Penelope decided it was unlikely that Beau passed through that way, she still wonders if maybe he ended up there. Maybe not at the same ramp as she did, but somewhere under the river, somewhere no one knows about.

She hasn't suggested it yet, but she has the distinct feeling that, when or if they run out of options and places to look, she will find herself back under the river. That, at least, would make sense to Frankie. If they lost Beau to the Styx, then they must turn back to the Styx for answers.

She touches the face of the medallion with the tip of her finger and then brings the finger up to her lips. Being dead for almost a year, she'd almost forgotten the taste of magic.

It tastes heavenly, like honey on her tongue, a sweetness she misses so deeply, she feels it in the soles of her feet.

Penelope shifts in her sleep, turning over so that the curve of her cheek is just visible in the low light of the room.

For the first time since Frankie died, she finds herself feeling somewhat hopeful about her future. Maybe, together, they can find Beau.

Maybe with Penelope, Frankie thinks, very quietly and in only half-formed words, she won't feel so alone anymore.

2: The Boy Who Looked into the Void

When Beau Astor wakes up, there are two questions echoing in his brain.

The first: "What happened?"

The second: "Am I dead?"

In any other situation, these two questions would undoubtedly cause unrelenting debate among philosophers and stoned college freshmen alike. However, they were completely rational questions because, for one, Beau Astor has been known to be a bit slow on the uptake. And two, he did indeed die.

Well, to be pedantic about it, he died on a boat on the River Styx while traveling from Souls Town to Death proper.

But when it comes to mind-bending and exceedingly rare metaphysical loopholes like the one Beau currently finds himself in, it's really the outcome that matters.

And yet, there is something else he needs to remember. Something important. Does it have to do with how he died? That does seem rather pertinent to his current situation. However, try as he might, and he tries mightily, the moments immediately preceding his death is a fog he can't penetrate.

He remembers being on the cruise ship, the *Danse Macabre* with its swan figurehead. He shudders. He never did like swans.

He was in Death, and yet, he was still alive. He remembers that much. He was most certainly a living, breathing human person without a touch of the necrotic about him at all (unless you count a somewhat overworked liver).

But where is he now?

Beau opens his eyes (he is glad that he still has eyes to open), and notes that he can definitely see himself, still in the clothes he was wearing on the boat.

But that's it.

All around him, everywhere, over and under, is blackness. Not like the kind of black of a room without light. It is pitch black in the way a starless sky would be black. It isn't dark, so much as an absence of anything at all.

There is nothing.

The most literal definition of "nothing."

It is just him, and that's it.

He had a passport, which guaranteed his ongoing breathing status in what was normally the afterlife for almost all sentient beings in that particular universe ("almost all," because, as Frankie told him once, casually, "reincarnation is a thing, if you're into it; the waitlist is atrocious though"). He searches his pockets now, feeling around for his passport, but finds only his lighter and a broken cigarette in the front pocket of his coat.

As Beau tries to collect his thoughts, one in

particular keeps popping up, and he mumbles it to himself in the nothingness.

"Where the hell am I?"

Not hell, a voice, deep and low, booms around him.

"Hello?" asks Beau, looking around frantically. The darkness stares back at him, static and dense.

Hello, replies the voice.

"Where are we?"

Not hell, says the voice again. *This isn't hell. That guy's a jerk*, clarifies the voice.

"So, where are we then?"

We're here.

"Where's here?"

I don't know, replies the voice honestly.

"Who are you, then?"

I am both place and thing and infinity.

"Do you have a name?"

Name?

"Yes, like, something people call you. My name is Beau Astor. What's yours?"

Oh! says the voice, suddenly not so loud and booming—but soft, friendly, almost like they are standing right next to him. *I'm the Void. It's lovely to meet you, Beau Astor.*

ACKNOWLEDGEMENTS

This book would absolutely not have been completed without the help of my husband, Paul Carrubba, who wrote several sentences. Odds are, if it's funny or amusing or an interesting historical reference, it came from him. He's the clever one; I'm just a hack.

ABOUT THE AUTHOR

J. Lynn Carr is a newly published author with a longstanding passion for writing. She holds a master's degree in Library Science and has worked as a freelance designer, blending her creative talents across various fields. Her work has been featured in Vulnerary Magazine and Folklore Review. Currently, she works at a library in Austin, TX, where she resides with her husband and their two beloved dogs, Milly and Freddie.